"You must go,"

she whispered shakily.

"In a moment," he agreed. "First, though, *chérie,* I want to be certain that your nightmares are gone."

"They are...."

"Let us make sure of it." He looked somber, very adult and mature. "The best way to stem a nightmare is to create an experience to supplant it. Do you not agree?"

"That depends ... on the experience ... you have in mind," she managed breathlessly.

"Something very innocent. Like you, *ma chérie,*" he added with a tender smile. "There is nothing to be afraid of, only a contact which will prove to you that innocence can be as arid as my desert."

As he spoke, he lifted Brianna from the pillow and smoothed the spaghetti straps of her gown down her arms....

Dear Reader,

This month we have a wonderful lineup of books for you—romantic reading that's sure to take the chill out of these cool winter nights.

What happens when two precocious kids advertise for a new father—and a new husband—for their mom? The answer to that question and *much* more can be found in the delightful *Help Wanted: Daddy* by Carolyn Monroe. This next book in our FABULOUS FATHERS series is filled with love, laughter and larger-than-life hero Boone Shelton—a truly irresistible candidate for fatherhood.

We're also very pleased to present Diana Palmer's latest Romance, *King's Ransom*. A spirited heroine and a royal hero marry first and find love later in this exciting and passionate story. We know you won't want to miss it.

Don't forget to visit that charming midwestern town, Duncan, Oklahoma, in *A Wife Worth Waiting For,* the conclusion to Arlene James's THIS SIDE OF HEAVEN trilogy. Bolton Charles, who has appeared in earlier titles, finally meets his match in Clarice Revere. But can Bolton convince her that he's unlike the domineering men in her past?

Rounding out the list, Joan Smith's *Poor Little Rich Girl* is a breezy, romantic treat. And Kari Sutherland makes a welcome return with *Heartfire, Homefire*. We are also proud to present the debut of a brand-new author in Romance, Charlotte Moore with *Not the Marrying Kind*. When the notorious Beth Haggerty returns to her hometown, she succeeds in stirring up just as much gossip as always—and just as much longing in the heart of Deputy Sheriff Raymond Hawk.

In the months ahead, there are more wonderful romances coming your way by authors such as Annette Broadrick, Elizabeth August, Marie Ferrarella, Carla Cassidy and many more. Please write to us with your comments and suggestions. We take your opinions to heart.

Happy reading,

Anne Canadeo
Senior Editor

KING'S RANSOM
Diana Palmer

Silhouette
ROMANCE™
Published by Silhouette Books
America's Publisher of Contemporary Romance

SILHOUETTE BOOKS

ISBN 0-373-08971-6

KING'S RANSOM

*Long Tall Texans
‡Most Wanted Series

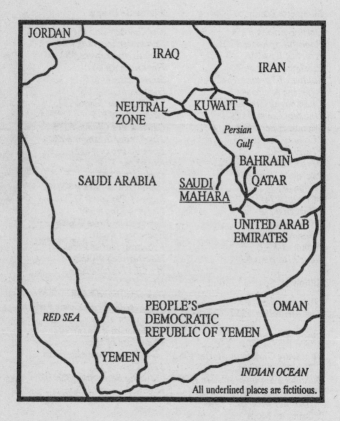

All underlined places are fictitious.

Chapter One

It had been the longest three weeks of Brianna Scott's life. She had enough trouble as it was, with her twelve-year-old brother in a coma. Tad had been in the unconscious state for three years, since the tragic death of his and Brianna's parents in an automobile wreck.

Brianna's fingers stilled on the computer keys as she fed a letter into the machine's memory. She didn't like thinking about how much longer Tad might remain in the coma. His full name was Timothy Edward, but he'd been Tad since he was born. She was ten years his senior, and she'd taken to giving bottles and changing diapers immediately after he was born.

Their mother had never been in very good health, and Tad's birth had been a major setback for her. Brianna had been handy around the house, thank goodness, or the advent of a new child into the family might have been a disaster. With Brianna's help, her mother was able to regain her health and take proper care of the little boy.

"You look thoughtful," Meg Shannon Ryker mused, pausing beside Brianna's desk with Daphne, her husband's secretary.

"I was just thinking about something," Brianna said. She smiled up at the lovely blond woman who'd married the top executive of Ryker Air only two days ago. It had been a stormy courtship, and a long-standing one, but the marriage hadn't really surprised anyone. The way Steven Ryker and Meg looked at each other was enough to set off major fireworks.

"I'm taking Daphne out for lunch," Meg said. "Can you cope?"

"As long as *he* isn't around," the younger woman said grimly.

"Steven took *him* out for lunch," Meg assured her. "He'll probably go right back to his hotel afterward. After the shoot-out he endured a while ago, it's a miracle that he's still alive. Steve and I can't even take a honeymoon until we get this mess straightened out."

"Aha," Brianna said merrily. "You hate him, too, don't you?"

"Not really." Meg chuckled. "He's very nice."

"Not to me, he isn't," Brianna said shortly. "He looks at me."

"You're very pretty, you know," Meg said, noting Brianna's exquisite complexion and big blue eyes in their frame of short, straight black hair.

"That isn't what I meant," Brianna corrected. "He…glowers at me. Glares at me. Stares daggers at me. *That* sort of looking."

"I see. Well, you did throw a paperweight at him," Meg pointed out.

"He insulted me," the younger woman muttered. "It wasn't my fault! I love barbecue. Everybody I know loves barbecue. How was I supposed to know that all his colleagues who were also cabinet ministers from Saudi Mahara were Moslems and they can't eat pork?"

"We didn't tell you, so we get to share the blame," Daphne offered, smiling. "I'm sorry. I meant to, but we got busy."

"We've never been so busy before," Meg agreed. "This new contract for Saudi Mahara's jets has been one long headache, although I certainly don't blame Ahmed for it. I'm glad we got the job. It means a stable budget for the company for years to come."

"I know that," Brianna said silently. "But…" Her eyes bulged. "Isn't that Lang?" she asked.

"Oh, Lord, don't let Steven see him," Meg squeaked, because she'd spotted the tall, husky government agent, too. Lang was well built, in his early thirties and handsome enough to turn heads. He was a wild man, though, and Steven Ryker didn't appreciate his devil-may-care attitude.

"What is he doing here?" Daphne wondered.

Lang noticed the three women staring at him. He moved toward them with a grin on his face that was reflected in his dark eyes. He was impeccably dressed in a dark suit, white shirt and conservative tie. The conservative look was a bald-faced lie. Lang was a law unto himself.

"I know, you can't resist me," Lang said, nodding. "But you're a married woman, now, Meg. Control those urges. Your husband already offered my boss a bribe to send me to Antarctica on a fact-finding mission."

"Inside a whale, if I remember correctly," Meg mused.

"Why are you here?" Brianna asked worriedly.

He evaded her searching gaze. "You'll find out soon enough," he promised. "I'm waiting for your husband," he added to Meg.

"Steven didn't mention that you were expected," Daphne said curiously.

"I asked him not to. We're very cloak-and-dagger about this," he explained. "No leaks. No loose lips."

"It's something to do with Ahmed, isn't it?" Brianna asked coolly. "Go ahead, tell me it isn't."

"He's trying to avoid being assassinated," Lang reminded her. "He's a foreign dignitary and we're sworn to protect him. We can't let somebody take him out here in Wichita. Bad for our image," he added.

"Can't you send him home and let his own people protect him?" she asked plaintively.

"Not really. Two of the ringleaders of a terrorist squad that we captured before they did him harm got loose on the way back to Saudi Mahara. Their colleagues have organized a second coup attempt in as many weeks. This is going to be one touchy issue until we resolve it."

"But I thought Ahmed was being sent home, too," Meg began.

Lang shook his head. "Too risky now. We've come up with a way to keep his identity secret and to protect him and his king. We're installing a man impersonating the king in the Hilton with armed guards on the whole floor. He won't leave his room, and if they make a try for anybody, he'll be first. He's one of our men, of course," Lang added with a grimace. "Getting the royal treatment. Lobster tails every night. Full breakfast served in bed every morning. I volunteered, God knows I did, I'd never have minded the risk. But they thought I was too eager," he said with disgust.

The women tried not to laugh. He flexed his broad shoulders. "Anyway, I'm going to have my hands full. Speaking of full hands, guess who just walked in?"

Steven Ryker and Ahmed ben Rashid were about the same height, both dark haired and dark skinned, but Steven's eyes were a light silvery color and Ahmed's face showed his Arab heritage. He had a mustache, too, unlike Steven. He smiled at Meg and Daphne, but the look he gave Brianna could have fried an egg.

She gave it back with interest.

"Daphne and I were going to lunch," Meg began.

"Go ahead, darling," Steven said gently, pulling her close to kiss her. "I can't turn loose yet. We have some business to discuss."

"You aren't leaving?" Lang asked Brianna suddenly.

She hesitated a minute, startled by the question. "Well, no, not yet...."

"Good." He turned to Steven. "We'd better get to it."

"All right. See you tonight, sweet thing," Steven told Meg, and the smile they shared made Brianna faintly envious.

She turned her attention back to her work, while Daphne and Meg called their goodbyes and Lang went with Steven on into the executive office.

"Yes?" Brianna asked Ahmed with a glare. "Did you want something?"

"You are obnoxious even before you speak," he said curtly. "In my country, you would live on bread and water forever with such an attitude."

"I'd rather live on bread and water than sit at an elegant table eating lobster with *you*," she said with smiling malice.

"As if you would ever receive such an invitation from me," he returned with faint contempt. "I have my pick of women, you see."

"The Sheik of Araby," she said under her breath.

"I beg your pardon?"

She lifted her eyes to his. "I do hope you enjoy your trip back home when you go, and the sooner the better."

He gave her an indifferent appraisal. "A woman with a tongue such as yours should welcome even the most casual conversation from a man. I am certain that you are unmarried."

"Yes, I am," she agreed happily. "Did my happy expression give me away?"

He frowned. "Give you . . . away?"

"Did it betray my state of unbridled bliss?" She corrected.

He didn't seem to find her comment amusing. "Women in my country delight in marrying and producing children."

"Women in mine don't have to get married and have children if they don't want to, or wear a veil, or join a harem, or become the property of their husbands," she replied sweetly.

He glared at her. "You are insulting. Such an undisciplined tongue will one day cost you any possibility of making a good marriage."

"One can only hope," she agreed with a sigh.

He said something in his own language. It sounded musical and insulting, and Brianna glared at him.

"Uh, Ahmed, could we see you for a moment?" Lang called, trying to avert a disaster.

Ahmed glanced at him and back at Brianna. He was standing stiffly beside her desk and reluctant to leave the field. The woman made him angrier than anyone in this country ever had. The death threats, the assassination attempts were all insignificant beside making this woman treat him with the respect that was his due. Women usually fell over themselves trying to catch his eye, get his attention. This one only insulted him, making a joke of his status. He couldn't remember feeling such rage.

"Ahmed?" Lang called again, more insistently.

"Oh, very well," the Arab said irritably.

Chapter Two

Brianna didn't see Ahmed again that day. But the next morning, he walked past her desk and gave her a look so icy that it made her shiver. She returned it with cold dislike as he passed through the office where she did her secretarial duties. If she disliked him, the reverse was also patently obvious.

Brianna found the tall Arab something of a puzzle, as many of the other employees also did. He'd been introduced as Ahmed ben Rashid, a cabinet official of the Arab republic of Saudi Mahara. But he had the arrogance of an emperor and a temper to match. She wondered if Lang was somewhere close by. The CIA was much involved in his protection, and there was something going on. Ahmed had been in the office just yesterday. Why was he back today? Wasn't it a risk for him to be seen in public?

If the bodyguard he carried around with him was any indication of the esteem in which his country held him, the United States government would do well to keep him safe, Brianna thought. But for her part, they could guard him on Alcatraz. She tried to imagine his regal presence sitting in a damp cell and her blue eyes twinkled with mischief.

"Nothing to do, Brianna?" Steven Ryker asked dryly from behind her.

She turned to face the president and CEO of Ryker Air, red faced. "Oh. Certainly, Mr. Ryker," she stammered. "I was just, uh, just, uh..."

"He doesn't like you any more than you like him," Steven pointed out. "The difference is that he hides it better."

"He doesn't, you know," she returned stiffly. "He called me names, he insulted me, he had me in tears...."

"You got even," he reminded her, smiling reflectively. "Do you have any idea how close you came to causing an international incident?"

"One can only dream, sir." She sighed, and smiled, pushing back her short black hair.

"You're hopeless," he murmured, laughing. "Stop glaring at him. He's one of our best customers."

"He's buying jet fighters to kill people with," she began.

He held up his hand. Since his marriage to pretty Meg, he'd mellowed just a little. "His government is," he countered.

"Same difference." She glared after the Arab's retreating back. "Why is he here again today?" she moaned.

"It's a secret," he said with an odd look. "But it has something to do with the fact that somebody blew up his jet last night."

Her eyes widened. "Who?"

"We don't know. Fortunately it was deserted at the time. The pilot was just on his way across the tarmac. But the government has decided to conceal him here until his people back home catch the two conspirators who escaped from custody. They think he may still be a target."

"Oh, brother," she said heavily, remembering all too well that Ahmed had almost been killed, and Steven and Meg and his private secretary along with him.

"The only good thing is that they don't know exactly what Ahmed looks like. The men who could have recognized him are in tight custody in Saudi Mahara."

"Are they going to take him to Washington to protect him?" she asked hopefully.

"Why would they want to do that?" a deep, amused voice asked.

Brianna and Steven turned to face the newcomer. It was dark, handsome Lang. The CIA man had saved

Steven's new wife from would-be kidnappers a short while ago, but Steven was still irritated at him because of the manner in which he'd saved Meg. Steven thought Lang was reckless.

"If it isn't the secret pain-in-the-neck agent," he muttered. "Hello, Lang."

"We meet again," the other man said with a grin. "Hi, Brianna, how about lunch? Or would you rather skip all the picky stuff and just get married now?"

She laughed. "You'd run a mile if I said yes."

"Probably. You could try and see."

"No, thanks. I have work to do."

"Indeed you do," Lang said, taking her arm. "Come along, Ryker. You're in on this, too."

"I am, but I don't like it."

"We've found the perfect place to hide Ahmed," he said, hurrying them toward Steven's office. "It's great. It's safe. It's the last place in the country they'd ever look for him."

"Where? Can I ask?" Brianna queried.

Lang paused at the closed door with his hand on the knob. "Why, in the bosom of his deadliest enemy, of course. Figuratively speaking," he added, and arched his eyebrows several times at Brianna.

She felt her jaw drop. He couldn't be thinking...meaning...

"Come in, and I'll explain."

Lang opened the door. Ahmed was standing at the window, his hands neatly folded behind him, his profile sharp and aristocratic as he gazed down on the parking lot below. He turned as Steven and Brianna came in with Lang, and his liquid black eyes made threatening flashes at her.

"Ahmed," Lang said brightly, "look who I've brought with me. It's your cousin by marriage, with whom you'll be living in your guise of a poor migrant cowboy."

Brianna pinched herself, but it didn't do any good. Ahmed glared viciously at the government man. Steven Ryker had to smother laughter.

"Stay with that she-cobra?" Ahmed asked haughtily. "I have told you already, I should rather live in the zoo!"

"That would suit me, too. You can stick him in the cage with the snakes!" Brianna said. She glared at Lang. "I live alone. I'm a single woman. I don't live with men. I don't like *him*. I especially would not live with him." She pointed at Ahmed.

"Everybody knows that. Which is why nobody will look for him at your apartment. And to make it even better, we're going to give him the credentials of a Mexican itinerant laborer, a cousin of yours from Chihuahua who just lost his job in Texas and needs a place to rest up and look for more work. Where better than with his favorite cousin?"

"I don't have any cousins from Chihuahua!"

"Now you do. Lucky girl," Lang added.

Brianna's fists clenched beside her neat gray skirt. She glared hotly at Ahmed's stiff face. "I don't even have male visitors. My reputation would be shot!"

"A relative can hardly be considered a blight on your reputation," Lang told her. "You'll be under constant surveillance, and you'll be safe. More important, so will he."

"No." She dared Lang to argue.

He moved closer, looking apologetic. "You have a twelve-year-old brother in a coma," he said quietly. "He's in intensive care in the local hospital and your insurance is about to run out. If the insurance stops, he'll have to be moved, and the specialized treatment he's been getting will also stop."

Brianna's heart climbed into her throat. "How did you find that out?"

"I'm a secret agent," Lang said calmly. "No secret is safe from me."

She drew in a rough breath, aware of Ahmed's curious stare. "What point are you trying to make?"

"If you help us, we help you. Ahmed's government is prepared to incur the expense of your brother's treatment, hospitalization and eventual rehabilitation if and when necessary."

It was almost too much to believe. Brianna moved to a chair and sat down heavily. All her worst fears were being brought into the light and vanquished. Tad was all she had left of her family. She adored him. It was like a miracle. Almost. Having to have Ahmed in her apartment was not going to be pleasant.

"Think about it," Lang advised. "Take a day or so to deliberate. Then we'll get back in touch. But we can't waste much time, you understand. If you refuse, we'll have to take other measures. That will negate our agreement to look after your brother."

Brianna winced. She couldn't refuse. Her brother's well-being was everything.

"If he moves in with me," she began, glancing uneasily at Ahmed, whose dark face was totally without expression, "how long will he have to stay?"

"Until we catch the two escaped assassins," Lang said. "We're pretty sure that they'll come here to Wichita and make a try for him. We'll be waiting if and when they do."

"What if they don't?"

"You'll have had the opportunity to learn a lot of Arab customs and your brother's bills will have been paid."

She lowered her eyes to the floor. She was going to regret this. Living with a man like Ahmed would be terrible!

"I'll be back in touch," Lang said when she was silent.

"I don't need to think about it," she said, raising her eyes. "I can't refuse. You knew it, too."

"I like to think I've planned well," he said, nodding.

"I won't be his personal slave," she added shortly, and her eyes shifted to Ahmed.

His dark eyebrows lifted. "God forbid," he said fervently. "I have very high standards for servants."

Her eyes narrowed. "And I have high ones for houseguests. I won't be imposed upon. You won't interrupt my routine."

He shrugged. "My requirements are few."

She didn't know why, but the way he said it made her uneasy. She had a suspicion that behind that tranquil expression, he was already plotting ways to upset her.

She was right. Ahmed moved in that very day, arriving with a virtual entourage of people carrying furniture, suitcases, trunks and other items.

Lang was with Ahmed, and two men accompanied him.

"This is great," Brianna said, glaring at all of them as she stood aside to let them into her apartment. Down the hall, doors had opened and two curious faces peered at the excitement. "Just great. Why didn't you hire one of those lighted signs to put outside the building and announce that you were moving him in here?"

Lang grinned. "Because we all look like poor working cowboys, don't you think?"

She stared at them intently. Well, they did rather look like working people. None of them was wearing a suit, including Lang, who was dressed in a pair of the most disreputable-looking, faded, tattered jeans she'd ever seen, with boots and a denim shirt. He didn't look like a secret agent at all.

Lang intercepted that curious look and grinned. "It's the latest thing in spy disguises. In this sleeve is a TV camera," he said, holding out a big, long arm, "and in the other is a miniature guided missile."

She glared at him. "What amazes me is that you still have a job at all!"

"Oh, they can't fire me," he said confidently. "I have an aunt in Congress and an uncle in the President's cabinet."

"I'm impressed," she said.

"So am I," he assured her. "I tell people about them all the time—especially my bosses in D.C."

"Why does that not surprise me?" she murmured.

He chuckled. Ahmed came in behind the rest of the load carriers and looked around disdainfully, with his lean hands palm down on his hips and a disgusted look on his mustachioed face.

"To think that I should come to this," he muttered haughtily. "By Allah, a tent would suit me better!"

"Not half as well as a narrow box would," Brianna began.

Lang dragged her off to one side. "Now, now," he soothed. "He's just not used to American apartments. You'll have to give him time to adjust. He'll get used to it."

"I won't," she assured him darkly. "Having to spend even a week with this man is going to require every thread of patience in my entire body!"

"There will be compensations," Lang promised. "Your brother's medical bills will all be paid, and you have to admit that it would be worth most any sacrifice to have that."

"It would," she had to agree. "You can't imagine how worried I've been—" She stopped and took a deep breath. "Tad's very special to me."

"Is that his name, Tad?"

"You know it's Timothy Edward," she mused, smiling knowingly at him. There wasn't much that got past Lang. "But I've always called him Tad for short."

"He's twelve, right?"

She nodded, averting her eyes. "He was so young when—" she paused "—when we lost our parents."

"Never give up hope," he said quietly. "I've seen miracles. Even the doctors admit that they still happen."

"I guess so. But after three years, hope dwindles."

He patted her on the shoulder awkwardly. "You might enjoy having our friend here for a while," he said. "He's not bad company."

She stared at him without blinking.

"Give it a chance, anyway," he coaxed. He glanced up at one of the men with him, who'd gone over the place with some sort of electronic equipment. "Anything?" he asked the man.

His colleague grinned and shook his head. "Clean as ice."

It was a small electronic instrument. Brianna glanced at Lang's sleeve with real curiosity.

"I was kidding about the TV camera." He chuckled. "And maybe exaggerating a little about the missile launcher."

"I saw a movie with one of those fiber-optic camera things," she remarked. "I was impressed."

"I'll wear one the very next time I come to visit," he promised with a wicked grin.

"What do I call him?" she asked with resignation.

"Ahmed?" He pulled out a brand-new ID card and a driver's license and passport and green card, all of which were intended to grace the pockets of her houseguest. "Pedro Rivera," he said. "Age thirty-four, native of Chihuahua, Mexico, occupation, farm laborer."

"Is he really going to work on a farm?" she asked hopefully. Her smile was evil.

"Ahmed?" Lang found that hilarious. "No, he's sort of between jobs, and he's depending on you to support him while he looks for work. He'll look very hard, we'll see to that. Applications in all major local businesses, and so forth."

"You could get him a job translating," she said.

"That would be tricky."

"Oh?" Her blue eyes were curious. "Why?"

"Well, he, uh, doesn't speak any Spanish."

Her face widened into a gleeful look of triumph. "None? None at all? How interesting! And he's supposed to be a Mexican laborer?"

"He said Spanish tastes terrible in his mouth and he refuses to learn it," Lang admitted with a grimace. "He speaks French quite well."

"Then why not let him pose as a Frenchman?"

"It would take too long to explain. Trust me," he added. "This will work. It's almost foolproof."

"Like the Titanic was almost unsinkable."

"Pessimist," he accused. "Think of the service you're doing your country!"

"By harboring a Middle Eastern cabinet official? How in the world does that help my country? I'm not

Arabic," she added coldly, glaring toward Ahmed, who was still muttering about his inferior surroundings.

"His country's strategic location makes it of great value to us," Lang explained. "The Middle East is a lighted stick of dynamite right now, with all sorts of factions fighting for control. We depend on oil from that part of the world."

"We shouldn't," she pointed out.

"I realize that," he said. "But the fact remains that we depend on foreign oil and we have to have it or our technology goes down the drain. We have to keep a lot of people happy overseas to ensure our continued supply. Ahmed is one of the people we have to keep happy."

"I thought his country had a king. Why don't we have to worry about keeping *him* happy?"

"If we keep Ahmed happy, it will keep *him* happy," Lang assured her.

She shrugged. "Okay by me. But for my money," she added, "they could boil him in oil and serve him on a bed of lettuce."

"What a mind. And you look so sweet," Lang commented dryly.

"I was sweet, until you and the Valentino clone over there invaded my life!"

Lang had to bite back laughter. He didn't dare show amusement, especially since Ahmed had overheard her and was joining them, spoiling for trouble.

"I beg your pardon?" he asked Brianna, and his liquid black eyes made her feel intimidated.

"I said, I hope you'll be comfortable here," she lied. "I'm going to cook my specialty for supper tonight."

"Not barbecue, please," Lang said out of the side of his mouth.

She gave him a speaking look. "Actually, I thought something Spanish might be in order. Chili, for example," she added, smiling at Ahmed, "with jalapeño peppers and refried beans."

"Ah, spicy fare," Ahmed said, smiling back.

She hesitated. "You . . . like . . . spicy food?"

"Indeed," he agreed readily. "I have no taste for bland meat."

She'd have to remember to cook him some unsalted spaghetti.

"Are we through?" Lang called to his cohorts.

"You bet!" One tall man came lumbering up. "Everything's in place—bugs, surveillance equipment, the works."

"You're going to spy on us?" Brianna choked.

"They might as well," Ahmed said haughtily, giving her an appraisal that spoke volumes. "Or were you hoping they might have something to look at?"

She clenched her small fists at her sides and forced thoughts of paid medical bills to the front of her mind.

"I'd rather eat nails," she assured him.

"No doubt you could, with a mouth like that," he agreed politely.

Lang got between them. "He's your adored cousin," he told her. "You love him. You're going to take wonderful care of him because your country wants you to."

"Then why can't my country live with him?"

Lang shook his head. "Believe me, I'd like nothing better," he said with a diplomatic smile in Ahmed's direction. "But I have some leave coming and I thought I'd go down to Texas and visit my brother and his family."

"Why can't he—" she pointed at Ahmed "—go down there with you? There are plenty more Mexicans in Texas than you're likely to find in Wichita."

"Oh, I'd hate to deprive you two of the opportunity to get to know each other," he said, tongue-in-cheek. "Think what it will do for international relations. Besides, my plans may change."

They stared at each other coldly. Lang moved out of the line of fire, motioning to his colleagues.

"Well, here you are, then," he said. "Nice and comfy, make yourself right at home. I'm sure Brianna will take excellent care of you."

"Are you?" Ahmed asked. "And what of my bodyguards?"

"They'll be around. So will our people," Lang said somberly. "Just don't take any unnecessary risks or deliberately make yourself a target. Mostly we'd like you to stay in the apartment while Brianna's at work. If you go out, mention out loud that you're going, and where. We'll have you trailed."

"This is outrageous," Ahmed said curtly. "I see no reason why my own bodyguard could not..."

"Because you're on American soil," Lang reminded him. "In this country, we're responsible for the welfare of foreign nationals. So be kind to government workers and let us do our jobs. Okay?"

Ahmed shrugged. He moved toward the window and stood there, looking out as if he felt too confined already.

"And don't spend a lot of time in front of the window," Lang pleaded. "You make an excellent target. We can't possibly watch every window in every building in Wichita twenty-four hours a day."

Ahmed moved back into the room, nodding his consent.

Lang was the last of the group out the door. "Well, I'll leave you to it."

"One moment," Ahmed called. "Who is going to unpack for me? I have no servants here."

Lang hesitated. He glanced at Brianna, who took up a belligerent stance that no one with normal perception could mistake. "Uh, well, we'll see about that later. Good day."

"I've been stabbed in the back by my own government," Brianna muttered once he was gone, her blue eyes spitting at her houseguest. "Don't expect me to help you push the knife in farther. I am not a servant. I do not unpack for my guests. You have two perfectly good hands. You can unpack for yourself."

He linked his hands behind him and stared at her. The intensity of the look made her very nervous, and she retreated to the kitchen. "I'll start working on something to eat."

He lifted the edge of a hand-crocheted doily and examined it. "I prefer shrimp cocktail for an appetizer," he remarked absently. "And with Mexican fare, I should think an aged Bordeaux would suffice."

She came out of the kitchen and looked at him. "Now listen," she said. "I do not have a wine cellar. I drink an occasional glass of sweet sherry or white wine, but I know nothing about vintages or which color wine goes with which food."

"A minor impediment," he said with a careless wave of his hand. "You can learn."

"I have no wish to learn, much less do I want a staggering Arab to put to bed at night," she added, pleased at the shocked lift of his eyebrows. "Furthermore, my budget doesn't run to shrimp cocktail. I make a good salary, but after I pay the bills, there isn't a lot left over for fancy food. You'll have to make do with what I can provide."

He sighed wistfully. "From caviar and Brie to this," he said in a long-suffering tone. "*Mon Dieu*, how are the mighty fallen."

She went back into the kitchen, muttering under her breath about how she'd like to fell him herself.

Chapter Three

Brianna went to the hospital to see her brother that night, leaving Ahmed complaining about the meager channels she had on her cable TV. He didn't ask where she was going and she didn't volunteer any information.

She sat by Tad's bedside, as she did most nights, watching the face that was so much like her own. His eyes were closed. But when they had been open, they were as blue as hers. It seemed so long ago now that Tad had laughed and played like a normal boy his age. She missed his mischievous personality. He'd been such a happy child. Why, oh, why had this to happen?

Sometimes she felt old when she sat with him. He hadn't wasted too badly. They fed him intravenously, and the nurses turned him and checked his vital signs to make sure he was getting what he needed to support his young life. Once the doctor had talked to her about shutting off the life support, but Brianna couldn't do it. She couldn't give up hope, not after they told her that his brain seemed to be functioning with some normalcy. She refused to quit. The last thing her mother had said to her, in the wrecked car, bleeding and gasping for air, was, "Don't let Tad die." It had been an odd thing for her to say, but Brianna hadn't forgotten. Tad was in no pain, and Brianna had hope. She couldn't give up.

She talked to him. She held his frail hand and told him all about her life, about her job, about what she was doing. She didn't tell him about Ahmed. It was the first secret she'd kept, but it would do him no good to know. She talked about the apartment instead and how she was going to redecorate the guest room for him when he could come home.

By the time she got home, tired and dispirited, Ahmed was in bed. She went into her bedroom and, on an impulse, locked the door. She was too tired to worry about having a man in her apartment and soon fell asleep.

When she got home the next afternoon, after a particularly long day, she was totally unprepared for the fierce thudding sounds coming from her bedroom. It sounded as if the whole place were coming down around her ears.

She got a bigger surprise when she made it to the door and discovered that he was supervising four dark men in business suits, who were putting away his clothes. In the process, they had unearthed half of Brianna's possessions and had deposited them in chairs, on dressers, and in the hall.

She dropped her purse in the middle of the floor and gasped, "What are you doing?"

"Making room for my things," he said from his lounging position in her best easy chair. "These quarters are hopelessly inadequate. That closet in the guest room barely holds all my suits. The other things must go in here."

"This is my room!" she wailed. "You can't move my things out!"

"I am your tenant," he said comfortably. "You must accommodate me." He stopped and called out something in curt Arabic. The men stopped what they were doing. One spoke for the rest in what sounded like an apology. Ahmed rattled off some more Arabic and made a dismissing sign with his elegant hand. The men went back to work.

"Tell them to stop," she said. "They can't do this. I have to have clothes to wear to work. I can't wear them all rumpled . . . !"

"Your clothes are hardly of any concern to me," Ahmed said, surprised. "It is my own appearance which is of prime importance."

She counted a long way past ten. It didn't help. "You get those men out of my bedroom!" she shouted. "And you follow them right out the front door!"

He ignored her. So did the men.

"You can't take over my bedroom!" she tried again.

"The guest room is inadequate. The bed is lumpy. I have no intention of sleeping on a lumpy bed."

"Then why don't you call the President and ask if you can stay with him at the White House?" she raged.

He considered that for a moment. Then he shook his head. "It is a bad time," he said simply.

She glared at him. She glared at the men. Everybody ignored her. She picked up her purse and went into the living room. At least he hadn't tried rearranging that yet!

The men left and he came sauntering out in a white-and-gold caftan with silver threads. He looked more foreign than she'd ever seen him look in the princely regalia. She hadn't considered before how alone the two of them were. The night before, she'd been to visit Tad and the sight of him had affected her much more deeply than before. She'd arrived late, and she hadn't seen Ahmed at breakfast. She'd gone straight in to work, thinking, silly her, that it was working out very well. Ha!

"You must do something about the television," he began. "There are too few channels. I want the French stations. Another thing, there is no fax machine here." He gestured impatiently. "How am I expected to attend to matters of state without a facsimile machine? I need a telephone line upon which these juvenile neighbors of yours are not always discussing—what do you call them?—arcade computer games!"

She just looked at him. He still didn't understand her budget. He made it more obvious by the day.

"And these...plants," he muttered, fingering the leaf of a philodendron with distaste and glaring at a trailing ivy plant, "they make the room feel like a rain forest. I prefer desert plants. They make me feel at home."

"I'll send right out for some stinging nettles and cactus," she assured him.

His black eyes narrowed. He had an arrogance of carriage that sometimes made him look dangerous. He was using it now. "You mock me. Few have dared that over the years."

"What will you do, cut off my head?" she challenged.

"I believe I...*we*...outlawed beheading some years ago." He waved his hand. "It was becoming politically incorrect with our allies. They found it offensive."

She couldn't believe he wasn't kidding. She moved toward the kitchen. "I'll fix something to eat." She turned. "No shrimp," she said. "And no wine. I had in mind some hot dogs."

"Hot...dogs?" His eyes bulged. "Hot dogs!"

"I like hot dogs with chili," she said.

"You served chili last night," he began.

"And I'm using up what was left tonight, on hot dogs." She sighed, exasperated, and frowned. "Don't you understand? I don't throw away food, ever! I stretch it. If I have leftover bread, I make bread pudding. I waste nothing! I can't afford to!"

It didn't register. "You have credit cards, surely."

"I owe up to the limit right now," she explained. "I just bought a new bed, for *my* bedroom," she emphasized, "because the mattress I was sleeping on was so lumpy. Until then, there wasn't a bed in the guest bedroom. Lucky you, not to have to sleep on the floor or the sofa!" she added sarcastically.

"I would never do such a thing," he said absently. "It would be unseemly. What is this limit? I have no limit."

"Why does that not surprise me?" she asked the ceiling.

He looked up to see who she was talking to, and she walked off and left him.

"I will have vichyssoise instead of hot dogs," he said. "I prefer cream and churned butter," he added with a smile.

She took down a boiler, filled it with water and put two hot dogs in it. She turned on the burner. Then she took a whole potato from the bin, walked into the living room and handed it to Ahmed.

"There you go. Instant vichyssoise. Just peel it and add cream and churned butter and a little water and simmer it for half an hour or so. Should be just delicious," she added, and walked right into her bedroom and closed the door with a snap.

When she came back, he was nowhere in sight. The potato was lying on the counter in the kitchen and the guest room door was closed. Her telephone had been unplugged and removed from the table by the sofa. She frowned, wondering what he could be up to.

Minutes later, he came back, carrying the telephone. He set it on the table and sprawled on the sofa.

"You might plug it back in," she suggested.

"Why?" he asked. "I unplugged it, after all, and plugged it into the bedroom wall. I am fatigued." He laid his head back on the sofa. "And very hungry. I had a hamburger from the corner diner for lunch."

He made it sound as if she should feel guilty about that. "With fries?" she asked cheerfully. "They make good fries."

"I loathe french fries," he informed her.

She'd mark that down mentally and soon she'd serve him some, she decided irritably.

She dished up her hot dog and added mustard and catsup to the bun she'd placed it in. "There's one left if you want it," she offered.

He glared at her.

She shrugged. "Starve yourself, then." She sat down at the table. Just as she lifted the hot dog to her mouth, the door buzzer sounded.

Ahmed got up and pressed the button beside the door. "Yes?" he asked haughtily.

There was a spate of Arabic, which he answered in kind, and pushed the door release.

"You can't do that! What if it's the people who are after you? They'll kill us all!" she raged.

He gave her a look. "It is my men," he told her. "Do you not think I know them by now?"

She started to argue, decided against it and went back to eating her hot dog.

Her peace didn't last long. An entourage of men in suits carrying boxes marched in, displaced her from the table with intimidating looks, and spread out a feast fit for a king for Ahmed. Then they left, without receiving a word of thanks.

He rubbed his hands together. "Ah," he said, inhaling the aromas of lobster and fresh sautéed vegetables and fresh-baked breads. He went into the kitchen, got a plate and utensils and proceeded to fill the plate. "You may join me if you wish," he added carelessly.

She glared at him and deliberately took a bite of the hot dog.

He hid a smile. Proud, he thought. It was an emotion of which he was not ignorant. She was no beauty, but she had spirit and compassion. Perhaps he would buy her a car when this charade was finished.

"You didn't thank your men for bringing all that to you," she remarked when she was washing up.

His face registered surprise. "Why should I? It is my fate to be served, and theirs to be my servants."

"You sound like a prophet quoting the Koran," she said. "I understood you to say that you were raised a Christian."

"I was," he agreed. "But I understand and respect the religion of my people," he added.

He turned his attention back to the exquisite cheese cake he was just finishing. "A most adequate meal," he said finally, getting up from the table to sprawl back on the sofa. The remains of his meal were strewn all over the table and the cabinet. Brianna, already tired, eyed the mess with distaste.

"You may clear away now," he said offhandedly.

"*I* may clear— *You* may clear!" she raged. "This is my home. Nobody orders me around in my own home! I'm not a servant!"

"You are my landlady," he said imperturbably. "And you can hardly say that I am not paying for my stay here."

That brought Tad back to mind. No, she thought, she couldn't say that. He wasn't paying, but his government was. She had to adapt to him. Perhaps it wouldn't be for much longer. The thought cheered her. She packed away the trash and washed up the few remaining dishes.

"I should like a cup of cappuccino," he murmured as he changed the channels on the television. "Sweet, but not too sweet."

"I don't know how to make cappuccino."

He turned, his expression one of amazement. "You cannot make cappuccino?"

He made it sound like a mortal sin. She shifted. "No." She hesitated. "What is it?"

"Cappuccino?"

"Yes."

"You are joking."

She shook her head. "Is it some sort of after-dinner drink?"

His expression softened as he realized just how unworldly she was. He got up from the sofa and approached her, noticing how nervous she became when he paused very close to her. "It is a coffee with frothed cream and cinnamon, very sweet. I am fond of it." He caught her arm, ever so gently, and held her in place.

"Oh. Well, I can't make it. I'm sorry," she added. His touch bothered her. How odd that it should disturb her so. She tested his hold and found him willing to let her break it. She stepped back and then looked up to see his reaction.

He was amazingly patient, almost contemplative, as he looked down at her. His black eyes mirrored his introspective mood, sweeping slowly over her exquisite bone structure, over her straight nose and down to her soft bow of a mouth.

"Women are property in your country, aren't they?" she asked, feeling chilled at the memory of what she'd read about some Arab nations.

"Not in mine, no," he replied. "We are a modern nation. There are those of our women who are not deeply religious, who consider the veil archaic and refuse to wear it. Our women work in public jobs and hold responsible positions in government." He smiled ruefully. "Needless to say, I am labeled an infidel by some disgusted neighbors."

"I expect your king is, too," she replied.

He cleared his throat. "Of course."

"Arabic is pretty," she said after an uncomfortable silence. "I have a friend who can speak a few words of it. It's musical."

"So they say."

"But it is," she argued, smiling nicely. "When you speak English, your voice has a lilt. It sounds very... intriguing," she said after a careful choice of words.

He lifted one dark brow. "Intriguing? Not sexy?"

She flushed, and he smiled again.

"Vous êtes un enfant, Brianna," he said quietly. *"Une très belle fleur avec les yeux comme la mer."*

She frowned. "I don't understand French," she said hesitantly, registering the depth and sensual tone of his deep voice as he stared at her much too intently for a mere acquaintance.

"It is just as well," he said wistfully. "Come and watch television with me."

"What are you going to watch?" she asked, because she knew already that it would do no good to demand access to her own television. He was being generous right now, but it wouldn't last. He didn't have it in him to be considerate for long.

"A special program on the connection between stress and the immune system," he said, surprising her. "It is a new study, one which has been challenged by many scientists. But I find the premise an interesting one."

She did, too. Her doctor often worried about her obsession with being at the hospital four out of every five days to sit with Tad. She never missed, even if it meant freezing or getting soaked, or waiting half an hour for a ride. He said that one day she was going to fall victim to some debilitating illness because of the strain. She never had, though. Not yet. There was a minor cold and a bout with the flu, but nothing more serious than that.

However, as she watched the program with Ahmed, she began to understand the connection they were trying to present. It was a little disturbing. Tad might be in a coma for the rest of her life. What then? She felt a surge of panic as she realized what she hadn't in three years—that she might never see the light at the end of the tunnel. It was the first time she'd considered that hope might one day be lost forever.

"This is not what I expected to see," he said suddenly. He changed the channel. "Illness depresses me. I had hoped for something scientific. Ah. This is much more pleasant." He left it on the public-television station, where a new Sherlock Holmes adventure was just beginning.

She was taken aback by his abrupt action. She couldn't find the right words to express what she felt. Illness depressed her, too, but she had no choice at all except to deal with it. She couldn't change the channel of her life to something more pleasant.

She watched the program with him, absently rubbing the edge of her blouse between her fingers. The blouse was getting frayed. She would have to scrap it before too much longer. That was disturbing. She didn't have much money for clothes.

After a few minutes, she realized just how tired she was. She got up from the sofa. "There's a bottle of cola in the fridge, if you get thirsty," she said.

"No Perrier?" he asked without looking away from the screen.

"Dream on." She sighed.

He didn't reply. She moved toward her bedroom, glancing back as she went down the hall. He obviously hadn't realized yet that he was going to sleep on that lumpy mattress in the guest room. He'd probably get the idea very soon. She wasn't giving up her brand-new bed.

She went into the bedroom and closed the door. Then she locked it and placed a chair under the doorknob. She nodded. *There you go,* she thought. *Get through that!*

Mindful of any hidden cameras, she turned out the lights before she disrobed. She was blissfully unaware that the agency had infrared cameras and film, and also that they were discreet enough not to bug her bedroom. Well, not with a camera, anyway.

Having donned her long gown and brushed her hair, she got into bed and pulled the covers up with a sigh. She was almost asleep when she heard the soft whine of the television cut off and footfalls coming down the hall.

There was a sudden stop, an exclamation, and then several loud words in Arabic at the door to her bedroom.

"You might as well calm down," she called through it. "I've double locked the door and there's a chair under the doorknob. It will take a battering ram to get in here. This is my bed, and I'm sleeping in it. If you don't like it, you can call somebody and complain!"

"You think that I will not?" came the haughty reply. "You will be surprised!"

"No, you will," she mused aloud. "Because no red-blooded American gentleman is going to try to force a woman to give up her bed."

She lay back down with a smile and closed her eyes. She didn't even feel guilty. He had no idea how hard and long she'd worked to afford this moderately priced new bed and mattress and box spring. He seemed to have no idea at all what things cost. Presumably his government fulfilled his every whim. It must be nice, she decided, to be in the diplomatic service.

If she'd thought she was home free, she was in for a surprise the next morning. He still wasn't up when she left, and she didn't leave him any breakfast. After his threats of the night before, she didn't think he deserved any. But her conscience plagued her all the way to work.

Once she got there, Mr. Ryker called her into his office. Lang was sitting cross-legged in a chair. He smiled as she came in.

"Oh, no," she pleaded. "Not you again."

"You'll break my heart if you keep talking like that," he complained. "And here I am to compliment you on the way you're taking care of your sweet cousin."

"He isn't sweet," she muttered. "He's a barracuda in a mustache. He commandeered all the closets and all my drawer space, and he even tried to get into my bed last night!"

Lang gasped. "Why, Brianna, I'm shocked!"

"Not while I was in it," she said impatiently. "I mean he tried to take over the master bedroom!"

"Yes, I know. He telephoned my boss this morning, early. He also telephoned the Pentagon, the Joint Chiefs of Staff and the Secretary of State. Not to mention," he added, "the Secretary of Defense." He shook his head. "You have no idea how much trouble you've caused."

"He didn't call all those people. He couldn't.. wouldn't!"

"He did." He smiled ruefully, pushing back a stray lock of dark hair that fell onto his broad forehead when he leaned forward. He rested his forearms over his knees. "In fact, I've been chewed out since daylight this morning. If you don't let him have the master bedroom, I'm afraid his government may declare war!"

She sat back in her chair, her face almost the color of the soft red turtleneck sweater she was wearing with her gray skirt. "I don't believe this."

"You'd better. I'm not even joking," he added solemnly. "This is a man who's quite used to getting everything he wants. He's never been refused in his life. He's rich and powerful and he isn't used to being denied—least of all by a young lady of your age and position."

"He's only a cabinet minister," she protested. "How can he have that much influence?"

"He has relatives in power in Saudi Mahara," he explained.

"Oh."

"We'll furnish you with a new bed for the guest room," he offered. "And a new vanity and a chifforobe. How about that?"

She hesitated. "Why not just let him bring a bed of his own to the apartment and sleep on that?"

"Great idea. We'll suggest it to him."

"Could you do it before I have to go home?" she asked. "I'm beginning to recognize several words in Arabic, and I don't think they're very nice."

"I can guarantee it." He grinned sheepishly at her start of surprise. "The bugs . . . ?"

"Yes. The bugs." She turned her head a little. "You, uh, you don't have any cameras in the bathroom or anything?"

He chuckled, noticing that Steven Ryker had put his hand strategically over his mouth.

"No, we don't. I promise you. We don't have cameras anyplace where they'd embarrass you."

She let out a long, audible breath. "Oh, thank God. I've been dressing and undressing in the closet."

"No need for that. None at all." He hesitated. "There's just one little thing. How did he get you to cook him vichyssoise and lobster?"

"But I didn't," she said. "I have no idea how to make those things. He had his men bring them in last night."

Lang was suddenly, starkly serious. "He what?"

"He had his men bring all that stuff in."

"Well, I'll be. You take five minutes to go to the men's room and look what you miss!"

"I thought you had the telephone bugged," Brianna said.

"I did. But Collins tripped over the wire and broke it. We were trying to make a splice.... Oh, never mind. Calling out for lobster, was he? Well, we'll see about that!"

Lang stood up, and he looked very angry. Brianna brightened. She wished she could go home and watch him give Ahmed hell.

She couldn't. But just the thought of it got her through the whole day, smiling.

Chapter Four

But when Brianna got to the apartment that night there was absolutely nothing out of the ordinary. Nothing very visible, at least.

Ahmed was sitting on her sofa glaring at the television, where a soap opera was playing. Two people were in bed, making passionate love. The sounds of it were embarrassing to Brianna, who sideskirted the sofa and went straight down the hall to her bedroom.

She took off her jacket and stretched, stiff from hours of sitting. As she turned, she noticed Ahmed in the doorway, watching her with eyes whose expression she couldn't define. She didn't know that the stretching motion had outlined her young body in the most sensuous, arousing kind of way. Or that Ahmed, a connoisseur of women, had stopped dead just to look at her.

"What is it?" she asked.

"They have removed the telephone directory and the information service does not function," he muttered. "This is your doing."

She grinned. "Yes, it is. Didn't I do good? Furthermore, I am sleeping in this very bed tonight and you are going to have a nice, new bed in the guest room. I did that, too."

"You did no such thing," he denied. "I have spoken to your friend Lang. He is sending over a bed. But it is you who will sleep on it. I am occupying this room as of tonight."

"You are not! This is my apartment, buster, and nobody kicks me out of my own bedroom!"

"If you do not vacate it, there will be an international incident of proportions which you cannot imagine," he countered smugly.

"You spoiled old brat!"

He gaped at her. "I beg your pardon!"

"Lang told me that nobody ever said no to you in your life. Well, it's time somebody did! You can't just walk in and take over. You have no right!"

"I have more rights than you," he countered. He folded his arms across his chest. The blue silk shirt he was wearing made his eyes look even darker. "Call Lang. Lodge a protest. He will not take your side against me. He will not dare."

"I don't give a frog hair who you are or what you do, this is where I live and I'm not budging!" she raged, her Southern drawl emphasized in anger.

He was frowning. "Frog hair?" He shook his head and muttered something in Arabic. "These frogs, they have no hair. Are you demented?"

"Yes," she answered him, "I am demented. That's why I allowed them to talk me into letting you stay here!"

His dark eyes sketched her angry face and lowered to the smooth, sleek lines of her body before they returned to capture her startled eyes. "How old are you?" he asked.

"That is none of your business," she said uncomfortably.

"I can find out."

"Go right ahead." She felt a little shaky. "Now, if you don't mind, I'd like to change before I have to start cooking again."

"Had you not complained, we could both be served with lobster thermidor," he reminded her.

"I don't like lobster," she muttered. "At least, I don't think I do. I could never afford any, even to taste."

He scowled. "You are paid a good salary."

"Of course I am," she agreed. "But it doesn't stretch to foods like lobster. I have a little brother in a coma, don't you understand?" she asked softly. "Every spare penny has gone toward his comfort, until now."

He seemed surprised. He moved a little awkwardly. "Yes, yes, I have heard about the boy."

"Well, he's more than gossip to me," she replied. "I took care of him after he was born, played with him, fed him, diapered him.... I had to, because Mother wasn't well for a long time. But he was a joy, not a burden. He's a smart boy," she added, hanging on to the good times for all she was worth, fighting the hopelessness and fear. "He'll get up out of that bed one day, and play baseball again...."

Ahmed was touched by her reluctant show of emotion. He found himself wondering about the boy, about her. He hadn't been curious before, but now he was.

"What do the doctors say of his chances for recovery?"

"They say as little as possible," she replied, having regained her almost-lost composure. "Medical science can't do any more than it already has. The brain is still very much an unexplored territory, you know. Comas are unpredictable."

"His has lasted long?"

"Three years." She moved toward the door and held the doorknob impatiently. "If you don't mind?"

He moved back into the hall and she closed the door. It hurt to think how long Tad had lain in the hospital bed, knowing no one. She was going to see him tonight, but like all the other nights, it would be an exercise in futility, in loss of hope. She was growing more depressed as time passed.

She changed into jeans and a loose, long-sleeved white knit shirt and socks. She didn't bother with her hair or her face. After all, Ahmed was not an invited guest whom she wanted to impress. He was, at best, a positive irritant.

When she reached the living room, he had the television blaring on the news channel. She ignored him and went into the kitchen to cook. It was going to be meat loaf tonight, she thought heavily. She was so tired of meat loaf, but it would stretch to two days. She glanced at Ahmed and wondered how he was going to like something that unglamorous.

"What culinary delight are you planning for this evening?" he asked with resignation.

"Meat loaf, mashed potatoes and green beans."

He made a terrible face.

"There's always soup," she continued.

He made a worse face and turned away from her to glare at the television screen.

"Why don't you call the CIA and tell them you're starving here? Maybe they'll find you a nice new place to live."

He didn't reply. He looked even more unapproachable than he usually did.

She went on with her chores, humming softly to herself. If he wanted to starve himself rather than eat what normal people did, that was just too bad.

"Think of it as an exploration of ethnic fare," she told him when she'd put everything on to cook and she was sitting in the big armchair by the sofa. "This is what Americans eat every week."

"No wonder your country is so uncultured."

"Uncultured?" she asked, affronted. "And what are you, Mr. Camels-in-the-desert-under-a-tent?"

He gaped at her. "I have no camels in a desert tent!"

"You know very well what I mean," she returned. "You live in a country full of camels and tents and deserts."

"We have cities," he said. "Opera, symphony orchestras, theaters. We have libraries and great universities."

"And sand and desert and camels."

He glared at her. "You know nothing of my country."

"You know nothing of mine," she returned. "Most of us have never experienced that rarified air you breathe when you're over here. Steak and lobster, five-star hotels, chauffeured limousines.... Do you think the majority of the people in this country know what any of that is?"

He scowled at her. "You do not understand. These things are my right."

"You have it too easy," she said curtly. "You should have to work for minimum wage and live on leftovers and drive a car that always sounds like it's got half a potato shoved up its tail pipe! Then you'd know how the rest of the world lives."

"All that concerns me is how I live," he said simply. "The rest of the world must cope as it can."

"What a selfish attitude!"

"There will always be people who are poor," he said philosophically. "Why should I deny myself because there are people less fortunate in the world?"

"You might consider doing something to help the less fortunate, like taking a cut in your salary and giving up some of the trappings of your luxurious lifestyle."

He drew up one long leg. He was wearing jeans, very tight ones, and she found the sight of him lounging on the sofa very disturbing. "My life-style, as you call it, is my heritage. I intend giving up nothing. However, I have done what I can for my own people," he said, ignoring her glare. "And your definition of poverty might find some resistance in my country. Our native nomadic tribesmen find their lifestyle satisfying and superior to the spiritual poverty which exists in our cities. They do not consider themselves poor, despite the fact that industrialized Westerners look down on them."

She frowned. "I don't understand."

"That is obvious." His dark eyes smiled faintly. "You think that because you have great machines and factories that you are superior to less developed peoples."

She hadn't considered the question before. "Well . . . we are. Aren't we?"

"Have you been to college, Brianna?"

She felt something flower inside her at the way he spoke her name. He made it sound musical, somehow. She had to stop and think to remember the question. "No," she replied. "I took some business courses to improve my typing and shorthand."

"When you have the time, and your circumstances are improved, you might benefit by a few courses in sociology and racial diversity."

"I suppose you have a college degree," she said.

"Indeed. I am an Oxford graduate."

"In . . . ?"

He smiled. "Science, with a major in chemistry and physics. My father greatly approved my choice. Our people were the founders of science."

"In that case, with such a background," she said impishly, "perhaps you could chemically create a lobster for yourself in the kitchen."

He frowned. Then the words made sense and he chuckled. The sound was very pleasant to Brianna's ears, deep and rich.

"Perhaps I could, given the right ingredients," he mused.

An item on the news caught his attention. He turned back to listen and Brianna escaped back into the kitchen.

After a few muttered comments about the lack of proper silverware and china and linen napkins, which made her glower at him, he settled down to the meal with surprised pleasure.

"I have not tasted such food before," he said. "It is good."

"You needn't sound so surprised. I'm not exactly hopeless in the kitchen. My mother was a wonderful cook. She taught me how." She lifted her eyes. "Does your mother cook?"

He laughed uproariously. "No. Her hands were never allowed to do anything so menial."

She felt reprimanded and flushed a little. "Yes, well, in America it isn't considered menial."

"I beg your pardon, I did not mean to insult you," he said surprisingly. "You are a good cook."

"Thank you."

He took a last bite of the meat loaf and sipped sweetened, creamed coffee with obvious pleasure.

"You said her hands *were* never allowed," she asked. "Is your mother no longer alive?"

"What a soft way you have with words, Brianna," he said with a curious smile. "Always the passive, not the active voice, when you ask something that might be hurtful." He put down his fork. "Yes, she is dead. So is my father. They were murdered."

She dropped her fork. It clattered against the inexpensive ceramic plate, the noise loud in the sudden silence. "Oh, I am sorry," she stammered.

"It was a long time ago," he said. "The sting is still there, but their murderers were caught and executed."

All that reminded her that Ahmed was himself a target of would-be executioners. She grimaced as she looked at his impassive face. "Aren't you afraid?"

"Why waste energy in such futility?" he asked. "I will die when my time comes." He shrugged. "It is our destiny to die, is it not, one day?"

"Well, if assassins were gunning for me, I wouldn't be quite so casual about it!"

He smiled. "You are a curious girl."

"Woman," she corrected.

He lifted an eyebrow, and his eyes were old and wise. "Girl," he replied softly.

She got up a little jerkily and collected the plates. "I made a cherry pie for dessert," she said.

"Ah. My favorite."

"Is it?" She was sheepish. "Mine, too."

"A thing we have in common. Shall we find more, I wonder?"

She didn't answer him. He was getting under her skin, and he frightened her in emotional ways. She wasn't eager to let him turn her life upside down.

They finished the pie in silence. He went back to the television while she cleared the table, washed up the few dishes and went to get her coat and purse.

"Where are you going?" he asked, looking at her over his shoulder.

"To see Tad."

He got up and turned off the television. "I shall accompany you."

"Now, wait a minute," she said. "They said you shouldn't leave the apartment."

He was putting on his coat, ignoring her. "They will know that I am accompanying you. They will be watching."

She threw up her hands. "I never saw a man so enchanted with his own demise!"

He joined her at the door, ignoring her cry. "Shall we go?"

She gave up. She could hardly restrain him. He was very tall, close up, and she imagined he was very fit, too, if those muscles she'd seen in his legs and arms were any indication.

"Do you work out?" she asked suddenly.

"In a gym, you mean? Not really. I ride my horses and work with them."

"You have horses?" She was impressed. "I love horses. What sort are they?"

"Lippizaner stallions," he said.

"Those huge Austrian ones? But aren't they terribly expensive?"

"Astronomical." He noticed her suspicion and chuckled. "They are the king's," he explained. "But he allows me to train them for him, during my spare hours."

"Oh, I see. How nice of him."

He looked very smug, and lights danced in his black eyes. "Indeed."

It wasn't going to be such a bad evening, she thought. He was in a good mood.

And it lasted just until they reached her little car. He stopped and gaped at its bruised front fender, its rust spots covered with Bondo in preparation for the paint job she was having done on the installment plan. It was going to be red one day. Right now it was orange and rust and gray. Its tires were good, though, and its seats were hardly ragged at all. There was the small crack in the dash....

"You expect me to ride in that!" he exclaimed, bug-eyed.

"It's the only car I own," she informed him.

"It is . . . pitiful."

She put her hands on her hips and glared up at him. "It is not! It's a diamond in the rough. Just because it isn't cosmetically perfect . . . !"

"It is a piece of junk!" he said harshly. "Why do you not buy something new, instead of riding around in this death trap?"

"Because it's all I can afford!" she countered proudly. "Do you think everybody can just walk into a car dealership and buy a new one whenever they feel like it? This is the best I can do, and you have no right to make me feel ashamed of my car!"

He started to speak just as a car pulled slowly up to the curb, a sinister-looking black one, and stopped in front of Brianna's car. She saw it and without even thinking, she suddenly pushed Ahmed against her car and tugged his head down, so that he was between the car and her body.

"What are you doing?" he exclaimed, fighting her hold.

"Will you be still?" she squeaked. "What if it's *them?*"

"The CIA?"

"The assassins!"

"Oh. Oh, I see." He chuckled. "How very flattering, Brianna."

"Will you keep your head down?"

His lean hands found her waist and gently pushed her away from him. "Brianna, look, *chérie.*"

He turned her face toward the black car, where Lang was lounging by the back fender. He seemed lazily amused.

Brianna flushed. She quickly stepped back from Ahmed and pushed at her disheveled hair.

Lang walked toward them. "Hello, little lady," he drawled. "I was just passing and saw you and your cousin here and figured you might like a lift. Having car trouble?"

"Yes, indeed," Ahmed agreed.

"Then I'll be glad to drive you two wherever you want to go."

Ahmed put Brianna in back and himself in the passenger seat beside Lang. She was still seething about Ahmed's insults. She loved her little car, dents and all. Arrogant jerk, she thought, glaring at the back of his head.

"Would you mind telling me how it is that I have a Mexican cousin when I'm very obviously of Irish ancestry?" she asked Lang irritably.

"By marriage, of course," he said, chuckling. He glanced at her in the rearview mirror. She looked flushed and Ahmed was unusually silent. "Did you think I was going to shoot him?" he asked, gesturing toward his companion.

"I didn't know it was you," she protested. "I just saw a big black limousine. Next time, I'll push him out in the street," she muttered under her breath. "He insulted my car."

"That is not a car!" Ahmed joined in the conversation. "It is a piece of tin with spots."

"How dare you!"

"Excuse me," Lang interrupted. "But where are we going?"

"To the hospital," Brianna said.

"I should have remembered. You go almost every night." Lang's eyes met hers in the rearview mirror. "How long do you think you can keep it up before you collapse?"

"I've managed for almost three years," she said tautly. "I'll manage for as long as it takes."

He didn't say another word, but his expression was stark. Ahmed sat quietly pondering what he'd learned of Brianna all the way to the hospital. It surprised him to discover that she intrigued him. It must not be. They were worlds apart. She was an innocent, as well. He must marry one day for the sake of heirs, but they would of necessity have to be by an Arab woman. These flights of fancy must be suppressed. They were unrealistic.

Brianna left Lang and Ahmed in the waiting room. She was allowed into the intensive care unit alone, where she sat holding Tad's frail hand and talking to him about the weather and her day, as she always did. His dark lashes lay on his pale cheek, his unruly dark hair falling onto his forehead as he slept in his oblivion.

"Oh, Tad, I'd give anything if you'd wake up," she whispered huskily. "I'd give anything I owned!"

But he didn't, couldn't, answer her.

Lang leaned back against the wall, watching her through the glass, with an uncommunicative Ahmed at his side.

"Torture," Lang said heavily. "That's what it must be for her to go through this every day."

"Is there no other family, someone who might share her burden and lighten it?" Ahmed asked.

"There's no one . . . just her and the boy."

He let out a long breath. "Nurses could be arranged, you know," he said. "Around the clock. The best in the country."

"Ahmed, nurses can't cure a coma," Lang said. "You know that."

"They might spare her," he returned, nodding toward Brianna.

"Do you really think she'd stop going to see him, even if you could put round-the-clock doctors in there with the boy?" Lang mused.

"No. You are right, of course, I was not thinking." His eyes lingered on the young woman. "She is fragile to look at. But underneath, there is great strength." He turned his attention to Lang. "Do you know something of how that came about?" he added, indicating Tad.

"There was a wreck," Lang said. "They were going on vacation. A speeding car took a curve too fast and hit them head-on. The car rolled. Brianna's father and the driver of the other car were killed instantly. Brianna's brother was knocked unconscious. Her mother was . . ." He hesitated. "Her mother was fatally injured," he said, sparing the other man the details. "She lived until the next morning. She died just before help came. If anyone had spotted the car even an hour sooner, she might have lived, but it went down an embankment and was hidden from the highway."

Ahmed moved closer. "Brianna was in the car all night?"

"Yes. Trapped. She had two cracked ribs and a broken hip. You may have noticed that at times she moves a little awkwardly."

"No. I had not."

"She was in terrible pain, and she'd lost some blood. But Tad was the worst. It took Brianna over a year, and therapy, to get past the nightmares."

Ahmed studied her in silence. "She has great courage."

"Yes. She's an extraordinary young lady."

"How old?" He stared at Lang. "How old is she?"

"She's twenty-two, I think." His eyes narrowed. "If you seduce her," he warned quietly, "I'll come after you. I don't give a damn about your status or company orders, I'll make you pay if you hurt her in any way."

Ahmed's eyebrows lifted. "You are smitten with her?"

"I am protective of her," Lang corrected. "She's my friend."

Ahmed smiled quietly. "She is a rosebud, waiting for the sun. I would be a frost to deny her the hope of blossoming," he said. "I am much more aware than you think of the consequences. I have no evil intentions toward her. In between battles, I find her charming company." He glowered at Lang. "You will not tell her this, of course. One cannot afford to parade one's weaknesses before an enemy."

Lang's rigid stance relaxed. He even smiled. "No, one can't."

Ahmed clapped Lang on the back. "Despite her enmity toward me, did you see how quickly she jumped to my aid when she thought you were an assassin?" he mused. "She delights me."

"As if that tin can would have stopped a bullet from even a small-caliber weapon." Lang chuckled.

"She knows nothing of guns or wars or assassinations," Ahmed said. "Nor shall she. I must make certain that she takes no chances on my behalf again. There could have been tragic consequences had it been a true attempt on my life."

The other man sounded resigned and somehow sad. Lang found his response to Brianna curious. Ahmed was a rake, in his own fashion, although he was curiously protective of Brianna.

"We're keeping a close eye on both of you," Lang assured him. "She'll come to no harm."

"She had better not," Ahmed returned grimly, and his dark eyes made a threat of their own as they sought Lang's. "I consider her welfare no less important than my own. You understand?"

"I do," Lang said with a slow smile. "But I wonder if you do?"

Ahmed scowled with curiosity, but before he could take Lang up on the odd statement, Brianna came out of the ICU, had a brief word with the nurse and joined the men at the door.

"Any change?" Lang asked.

She only shook her head, her eyes lowered. "Can we go?" she asked dully. "I'm very tired."

Chapter Five

Brianna didn't sleep well that night. The black limo, the hopelessness of Tad's condition, the arguments with Ahmed were all combining to make her emotions a wreck.

At least the nightmares hadn't come back. She got up the next morning feeling drained. For once, Ahmed was awake. She found him in the kitchen in that long, foreign-looking caftan he lounged in, trying to discover how her coffeepot worked.

"I'll do that," she said, and moved uncomfortably when his dark eyes slid over her slender figure in her nightgown and pink robe. She was perfectly decent, except for her bare feet. She wondered why he should be staring at her so.

"You should dress first," he told her quietly. "It is unseemly for a maiden to appear before a man in her night clothing."

"Oh, I can't do it, but it's all right for you?" she challenged, indicating his caftan.

He smiled slowly. "Yes."

"I can wear my nightclothes in my own apartment if I want to," she informed him.

He moved closer. It was a sort of movement that Brianna had never experienced before, sensual and predatory and faintly threatening. His eyes didn't move from her face, didn't blink, and all the expression left his features. The only thing alive there was the growing dark glitter of his eyes.

"I'll, uh, just get dressed, why don't I?" she stammered, and ran for it.

When she came back, he was dressed, too. She made breakfast and he ate it without complaint. He gave no indication that anything out of the ordinary had happened. But Brianna tingled all day remembering the look in his eyes.

When she came home that afternoon, it was to find Ahmed sitting on the top step in her apartment house. He was playing with a Slinky, a small, dark-haired little boy sitting beside him.

"Again," the child pleaded.

"Oh, my aching back," Ahmed groaned comically. "You mean I must do it still again and chase this coil of wire down the steps?"

"Yes!" The child laughed.

Ahmed chuckled. "Very well, then. But this is the last time.'"

"Okay."

The Slinky came slowly down the steps, picked up speed and toppled right at Brianna's feet.

Ahmed came down behind it, spotted her and smiled as he retrieved it. "We were having a bit of fun," he explained.

"So I see. Lang won't like it."

"What he doesn't know won't bother him," Ahmed informed her. He handed her the Slinky. "My friend Nick will let you play, if you like. Won't you, Nick?" he asked the little boy.

"Sure!"

Brianna smiled at the child. "And you know I'd love to. But I have to feed my cousin."

"Aww, Pedro isn't hungry, are you, Pedro?"

"Pedro" grimaced. "Well, my boy, actually I am, a bit. Do you mind? We can do this again sometime."

"No, we can't," Nick wailed. "I have to go stay with my grandma for a week. We're leaving as soon as my dad gets home."

"I am truly sorry," Ahmed told him. "I have enjoyed our games."

"Me, too. Will you come back and see me again sometime?" Nick asked, his big eyes pleading.

Ahmed smiled, smoothing over the dark hair. "Sometime," he agreed.

"Okay, then." He ran back up the stairs, making plenty of noise.

Ahmed led the way up the stairs to Brianna's apartment and held the door open for her.

"You like children," he observed.

"Very much."

"You should marry, and have some of your own," he told her.

"I have Tad to look after," she said evasively. "I need to change."

He stopped her, without touching her at all, just standing in front of her so that she couldn't get past him. "There is something more, something deep," he said, searching her evasive eyes. "You have no desire to marry. I can see it in your face."

"We're not all cut out for marriage." Her face was flushed. "Please. I have to change."

His lean hands gently closed on her thin shoulders. "Tell me."

She closed her eyes. He was impossible this way, so tender and compassionate that he seemed almost another man entirely. "I can't," she whispered. Her big blue eyes opened straight up into his. "Please let me go!"

He accommodated her, standing back. "As you wish," he said quietly.

She went quickly into the bedroom and closed the door. She leaned back against it, her face twisted in anguish, her lip very nearly bitten through. Why did he have to ask questions that hurt her? she wondered. Why couldn't he just mind his own business!

She started to go into the kitchen, as she did every day, when he stopped her.

"Lang has reconnected the telephone," he murmured dryly. "And I have taken advantage of the situation. Wait."

"You haven't ordered out again?" she said nervously. "It's taking too big a chance, even I can see that!"

"My own men are attending to my needs," he said simply. "There is no risk of infiltrators."

"The neighbors here are not blind," she said, exasperated. "How is a poor Mexican laborer affording all that expensive food? People will wonder!"

He scowled. "Poor Mexican laborer?" He echoed her words.

"You!"

He shifted, as if he found the description distasteful. "I cannot live on hot dogs," he said curtly. "I did enjoy the meat loaf and vegetables, but I am accustomed to richer fare."

"You'll die of high cholesterol and gout," she accused.

His eyebrows arched. "This from a woman who is contemplating a meal of hot dogs, which ooze cholesterol?"

"I like hot dogs!"

"And I like quenelles of sole and sautéed asparagus with crepes flambé for dessert," he replied.

"Your poor starving people," she muttered. "Do they know that you're eating like a king while they chew on cold mutton in their desert tents?"

He pursed his lips. "Most of them eat couscous and lamb curry," he replied. "And semolina. Cold mutton is hardly appealing."

"I was making a point."

The knock at the door spared him an answer. He let his men enter the apartment, laden as they were with cardboard boxes of uncertain origin.

None of that looked like expensive food. It looked like the contents of a yard sale.

Ahmed grinned at her. "Disguised cuisine," he said. "Don't you approve?" He threw orders at the Arabs, who dispersed the contents of the boxes onto the table and left the apartment minutes later.

"Lobster tails," Ahmed indicated. He obtained a fork, speared a morsel and held it to Brianna's startled lips. "Taste," he said gently.

She took the bit of lobster into her mouth, disconcerted by the way Ahmed's attention suddenly fell on her lips as she savored it.

"It's... very nice," she said uncertainly.

"You have a flake of it on your chin. Be still." He took it on the tip of his finger and offered it at her lips. Holding her eyes, he eased it onto her bottom lip, but the movement of his fingertip was suddenly very sensual. He nudged it past her teeth and into her mouth and watched with pleasure the way her cheeks flushed and her breathing changed.

The tip of her tongue encountered his finger. She jerked back, and she saw the expression in his eyes darken and threaten. With her last instinct for self-preservation, she stepped away from him, shaken.

"Thank you for the taste," she whispered. "But I think I still prefer hot dogs."

"As you wish."

He was finding it hard to breathe and act normally. He should not have touched her. It would make things worse.

She fixed herself a hot dog and opened a small bag of potato chips.

"Even more cholesterol," he said, pointing at the potato chips with a forkful of chive-and-butter-and-sour-cream-choked potato.

"Look who's talking," she returned.

He chuckled. "You have spirit."

"Around you, I need to have it," she muttered.

He finished the potato and pushed the plate containing it and the remains of his lobster away. He retrieved the crepe with its exquisite fruit filling and nibbled at it. "Would you care to sample this?" he asked.

She flushed, remembering her earlier weakness. "I don't like sweets, thanks," she lied.

He didn't reply. She was suddenly very transparent and he felt a weakening in himself that he didn't like. Lang was right. Involvement with Brianna would be tragic.

The nightmare she'd staved off for two days came that night. She hadn't gone to see Tad, because there was such a terrible rainstorm. The thunder and lightning frightened her, but she pulled the covers over her head and tried not to notice them. Clad in her silky green gown, because it was an unusually warm night for autumn, she lay stiffly until the worst of the lightning abated and she fell into an uneasy sleep.

But the nightmare came to replace the storm. She was trapped in the car. Her father was dead. She could see his face. Her mother's pain was vocal, almost visible. She begged Tad to wake up and talk to her. She begged Brianna not to let him die, not to let them kill him. Her voice went on and on, while Brianna struggled with pain that racked her in agony. She had to get out, to save her mother. She had to get out, but her mother cried out and the light went out of her eyes....

"No!" she screamed, fighting the hands that were trying to lift her, to save her. "No, no, no! I won't let her die...!"

"Brianna!"

She felt the whiplike movement of steely hands on her upper arms and her eyes opened by reflex. Ahmed was sitting on her bed, his face solemn in the light of the lamp by the bed. He was wearing some sort of silky dark pajama bottoms, but his broad, hair-covered chest was bare. He looked out of place in her frilly bedroom.

"Brianna, talk to me," he said, unconvinced that she was completely awake even now.

"I'm...all right. It was the nightmare," she whispered, shivering.

"You screamed. I thought the nightmares were a thing of the past," he added.

She didn't know that Lang had told him about the wreck. She sought his dark eyes. "They were," she said dully.

His gaze drifted over her face and down to the deep cleft of her breasts under the opaque lacy bodice of her gown. She hadn't realized before that the lace left her dark nipples quite visible. But then, nobody had ever seen her in the gown before.

Her hands began to lift, because his rapt gaze was disturbing. Her nipples went suddenly hard, tingling with unknown sensations, and she blushed at the blatant evidence that would tell him how much he affected her.

"Beautiful," he said gently, watching them change. "They are as the blush of dusk on the rose."

Her hands paused in midair. She watched him, puzzled, curious.

He looked into her soft, puzzled eyes. "Has no man ever described your body to you before?" he asked quietly.

"No one...has seen it," she began huskily.

His brows jerked. His eyes went over her again, appreciating the creamy satin of her skin above the gown, at the pulse in her throat, at the soft swell of her lips. He hadn't touched her. He only looked.

That was enough. He made her afraid. She didn't understand the feelings he engendered. She wasn't sure that she liked them.

"You must go," she whispered shakily.

"In a moment," he agreed. "First, though, *chérie*, I want to be certain that the nightmares are gone."

"They are...."

"Let us make sure of it." He looked somber, very adult and mature. "The best way to stem a nightmare is to create an experience to supplant it. Do you not agree?"

"That depends ... on the experience ... you have in mind," she managed breathlessly.

"Something very innocent. Like you, *ma chérie*," he added with a tender smile. "There is nothing to be afraid of, only a contact which will prove to you that innocence can be as arid as my desert."

As he spoke, he lifted her from the pillow and smoothed the spaghetti straps of her gown down her arms.

"You mustn't!" she protested when she realized what he meant to do.

But he pulled her face into his throat and continued, pushing the gown to her waist. Then he slid his lean, warm hands around her bare back and began to move her bare, hard-tipped breasts against his hair-roughened chest. She gasped. The sensation was beyond her understanding. It made her breasts swell, her body swell. There was a sudden uncomfortable tautness in her lower body, a rush of heat. Her hands stiffened where they rested on his bare shoulders, feeling his strength.

"Relax," he whispered at her ear, his voice lazily sensual, amused. She was like a tightly coiled spring, but her breasts were exquisite. He liked their softness, their hard little points digging into his muscles as he teased her body with his. "Do you like it?" he

breathed, letting his hands slide under her arms now, to brush her from side to side with damning sensuality.

Her nails were biting into him unconsciously. "You must...stop," she stammered, shivering as his thumbs worked onto the soft swell of her breasts and began to caress them.

"Only this, I promise," he whispered. His teeth nibbled gently at her earlobe. "Nothing to compromise you, nothing to shame you. Let me touch you, Brianna."

Her voice broke. His touch was maddening. He made her want shameful things. She shivered, and despite her reluctant mind, her body drew away to give him complete access to her breasts, while her face burrowed, ashamed, closer against his warm throat.

"No, no," he coaxed, lowering his mouth to her tightly closed eyes. "Do not be ashamed to enjoy what I can give you. I mean you no harm." His mouth pressed hungrily at her temple while his fingers trespassed onto the fullness of her breasts and traced patterns that made her writhe before they came to rest over the hard tips of her breasts.

She clung to him, biting her lower lip almost through, letting his hands caress her while his thumbs· and forefingers molded her nipples until her whole body ached.

"You delight me," he whispered roughly. He moved, sliding his exploring hands up and down her silky back in lazy sweeps while he held her nakedness against him once more. She could feel the thunder of his heartbeat shaking them both, and she hadn't the will to ask him to stop. She wanted it to go on and on, to never end. She hadn't known that there could be such joy in a man's touch.

She didn't know that her hands were in his hair until she felt him gently remove them. He lifted her away from him and laid her down against the pillow firmly, his hands on her wrists while his glittering eyes dropped to her bare breasts. The next step, she knew, would be to let him peel the rest of the gown away. She would feel his eyes on her, and then his hands, and...

"No!" she gasped. If he did that, he would see her hip. She couldn't bear for him to see it!

He was incredibly perceptive. He knew that she wasn't protesting the thought of his eyes on her body. He had a good idea, from what Lang had said, why she was so reluctant.

"Which hip is it, *chérie?*" he asked softly.

She stopped moving and stared up at him, red-faced.

"Which hip?"

She hesitated. "The ... the left."

He smiled apologetically, and with slow, gentle hands, moved the fabric of her gown down over her hips and discarded it.

She lay frozen while he moved the elastic of her briefs to give him a full view of the damage that had been done in the wreck. There were scars against the smooth flesh, from the injury as well as the surgery that was needed to repair it. She held her breath, almost afraid to look at him.

But when she did, his eyes were gentle, patient. "Ah," he said softly. "Is that all?"

She shivered, in relief mingled with uncertainty.

"Brianna, such a body is a gift of the gods," he said very quietly. "A few small scars are of no consequence, except as marks of bravery and sacrifice. You are exquisite."

She felt odd. Embarrassment should have overcome her, but she didn't feel it. She searched his eyes with curiosity, wonder.

"And now there will be no more nightmares, yes?" he asked softly, smiling. "You will sleep and dream of my eyes upon you."

Heat burned into her cheeks. He smiled. "This is shyness," he said, tracing the redness across her cheekbones. "It delights me."

Without awkwardness, he pulled her gown back up and replaced the small straps on her shoulders. He bent and brushed his lips gently across her closed eyelids. "You have given me a gift of which you are truly ignorant, are you not?" he whispered. "You have invited me to be your first lover."

"I . . . didn't mean to," she replied uncertainly.

He lifted his head, and his eyes were tender. "Nothing would give me greater pleasure," he said with sincerity. "But we are fated for different roles in life than to be together. I would take your innocence only if I could offer you the future. I cannot."

He was closing a door. She felt sad, but it was nothing she hadn't known already. She had Tad, and Ahmed was from another country, another culture.

Her hand lifted to his face, hesitant, until he carried it the rest of the way. She traced his wide, firm mouth, his mustache, his high cheekbones and the thick ridge where his dark eyebrows lay. His hair was thick and black and cool to the touch. She found him devastating, as dozens of women before her must have.

He took her palm to his lips and savored it. His heartbeat was still visible. *"Bonne nuit, ma chère,"* he whispered.

"I don't understand," she began shyly.

"You don't understand what?" he teased. "French, or why you permitted me such a liberty?"

"Both, perhaps."

"You are very young," he said. "Curious and shy. I find it a disturbing combination. One day, a man will carry you to bed in his arms and you will learn that a scar means nothing to a man in love."

He put her hand back down and pulled the covers over her. "Sleep well."

"You, too."

He turned out the lamp and rose from the bed, tall and suddenly dear. He paused before he closed the door to look back at her with an inscrutable expression.

Brianna slept. And there were no more nightmares.

There was a new familiarity and an equally new tension between Brianna and Ahmed after that night. He made certain that he never touched her, nor did he refer to what had happened. Brianna could have believed from his behavior that it had never happened at all. For her own peace of mind, she supposed that she should try.

But he was tense and he became more so as the days passed. Lang discovered that he was still having food imported, and a confrontation rapidly ensued.

"I cannot live on oblong orange containers of meat of mysterious origin wrapped in buns!" Ahmed raged, waving his hands expressively. "I have a palate, which is unaccustomed to common fare!"

"Hot dogs are no worse for you than that high-priced cream-covered slop you eat!" Brianna shot back.

Lang looked heavenward for guidance. "Look," he said, stepping between them to face Ahmed, "you have to cooperate with us or we can't protect you."

"It is my own men who have been importing food for me," Ahmed informed him. He was as tall as Lang, although not quite as husky. He was formidable looking, just the same. "They have brought it in plain brown boxes, and not in their suits or native dress."

"Yes, but the restaurant where they're getting the food is a public place," Lang argued. "They've been seen coming around to the back laden with cardboard boxes. The police are watching them. They think they've stumbled onto a smuggling operation!"

Brianna hid her face in her hands and choked on laughter.

Ahmed was unamused. "You might enlighten them," he advised Lang.

"I have," he said irritably. "At considerable expense to my skin. They didn't take kindly to being left in the dark about the circumstances of your stay with Brianna."

"That is hardly my concern," the Arab said with cold hauteur.

"It should be," Lang countered. He paused, rubbing his hand over his chin, the other hand jammed into his pocket. "You're one major headache."

"If I were in charge," he informed Lang, "I should draw the assassins into the open and deal with them myself."

"We'd love to," Lang returned curtly. "But we have no idea where they are right now. We've searched the city, but we can't unearth them. We're fairly certain that they haven't made it into the country yet, although they were spotted on the Yucatán coast earlier this week. Meanwhile, it would be of great benefit to you, and to us, if you could be a little more discreet!"

Ahmed shrugged. "I have been discreet."

"Stop importing exotic food!"

"Tell her—" he pointed at Brianna "—to stop shoving oblong orange containers of suspicious meat wrapped in buns at me!"

"Hot dogs," Brianna corrected. "They're hot dogs!"

"Brianna, if we bring you some groceries, can you cook him something else?" Lang asked, trying to compromise.

"Bring me some mushrooms," she said with a venomous smile, "and hemlock and beef steak. I'll fix him a meal he'll never forget!"

"You can't poison foreign dignitaries," Lang explained patiently. "They have to be carefully handled."

"Spoilsport!"

"We'll get something right over," Lang promised Ahmed. "Now, will you please leave the catering bit alone?"

Ahmed was reluctant. "I suppose that I could. She is a passable cook," he added without looking at Brianna.

"I'm a good cook," she retorted.

"Make an apple pie with whipped cream, and I'll join you for supper," Lang said.

She smiled at him. "Would you, really? Bring me some apples and whipping cream, then."

He chuckled. "I'd be delighted."

Ahmed moved between them. "A bad idea, I'm afraid," he told Lang. "You have been seen by most of the terrorist group. It would hardly be politic for you to be seen here."

Lang grimaced. "He's right," he told Brianna sadly.

"I can save you a piece of apple pie," she said with a defiant look at Ahmed.

"That's a deal. Well, I'll say so long."

She walked him to the door, aware that Ahmed was watching every move she made. She felt a new tension and wondered why.

"Watch out for him," Lang said, nodding toward the man in the distance. "He's a ladies' man, and you'd be a whole new experience for him."

She smiled at him. "Thanks, Lang. But I'm not totally stupid. I'll be fine."

"Okay. Take care."

"You, too."

She closed the door behind him, grateful that she was able to keep her expression blank. It wouldn't do to let Lang see that Ahmed had already discovered her for himself. She felt shaky inside remembering the feel of him against her. She couldn't afford to feel like that, either. This was just a passing experience. She had to remember.

She went back into the apartment and forced a smile. "How about a cup of coffee?" she offered brightly.

"Lang is attracted to you," he said shortly. "He leads a dangerous life, and he will not easily give it up."

"I know that." She was shocked. "I have no interest in Lang, except that he's very sweet and I like him."

He stared at her for a moment. Then he relaxed and turned back to drop onto the sofa. "I would enjoy a cup of coffee."

"Thank you," she prompted.

He frowned.

"Thank you," she repeated. "It's courteous to thank people when they offer to do things for you."

Ahmed continued to frown.

"A little courtesy makes people feel of value," she continued. "You might try it."

He hesitated until she went into the kitchen and started the coffee. But when she put it on the table, he looked up.

"Thank you," he said stiffly.

Brianna smiled. "You're welcome!"

Chapter Six

Lang didn't show up that night when Brianna went to see Tad, and Ahmed insisted on accompanying her. That meant he had to be crammed into the passenger seat of her tiny vehicle, and he complained all the way to the hospital parking lot.

"If you hate my poor little car so much, why insist on coming with me?" she asked angrily.

"Because it is dangerous for a woman to be outside after dark alone," he said, "in any city."

He was concerned for her. The realization made her feel warm inside, protected. She stared at him, entranced.

He touched her face lightly, aware that she was creating a sort of weakness in him. She pleasured him.

He withdrew his hand with reluctance, noticing that she had leaned closer involuntarily, trying to maintain the light touch.

"You disturb me, Brianna," he said huskily. "It is a weakness which I can ill afford. Come."

He unwound himself from the seat and waited for her to get out. He escorted her to the hospital with a firm hand under her elbow. But before they got to the front door, his hand had begun to slide down until his long fingers could intertwine sensuously with hers.

She stopped, aware of explosive sensations caused by his touch. He looked down at her, his jaw taut as the same feelings worked on him. His fingers contracted around hers, pressing his palm hard against hers, and for long minutes they stood on the sidewalk under a streetlight and simply stared at each other.

"This is unwise," he said, his voice deep and husky. But he moved closer, so that his body was right up against hers.

"Yes." She laid her cheek slowly on his chest, over the trench coat, and listened to the hard, heavy beat of his heart.

His hand freed hers. His arms came up, slowly, and around her. He drew her close and bent his dark head over hers. He rocked her gently against him in the damp darkness and wondered at the peace he felt.

When he let her go, she was hard-pressed not to wobble on her feet. She clung to his hand as they went up in the elevator. She left him reluctantly to go see Tad.

He waited, his eyes unseeing as he stared at the carpeted floor. Brianna was becoming too important in his life. He wasn't sure he could let her go when it became necessary. How odd that she'd managed to instill feelings in him that all the experienced women of his acquaintance couldn't. He felt tenderness with her. It was a new feeling entirely, for him to feel tender toward a woman.

When she came back, he was more disturbed than ever. He took her hand and led her back to the car, gently helping her into the driver's side before he got in beside her.

"How is he?" he asked.

She shook her head. "There's no change."

She started the car and drove back to her apartment. This time when they got out, he kept a distance between them. When they entered her apartment, he excused himself with a plea of fatigue and closeted himself in the guest bedroom.

Brianna was surprised by his sudden change of attitude. She hadn't known what to expect from him, but this certainly wasn't it. He seemed suddenly distant and unwilling to let her near him.

The next morning, when she dressed and went to fix breakfast, she overheard him speaking to Lang on the telephone. What he was saying stopped her in her tracks, out of sight in the hall.

"I tell you, I cannot stay here!" he raged. "The situation is becoming unbearable. You must make other arrangements." There was a short pause while he listened. "Talk to them, then, but I expect solutions, not excuses!"

He slammed the telephone down and Brianna retreated to her room, almost in tears. So it was like that, was it? He couldn't bear to be around her anymore. Was he afraid that she was going to embarrass him by falling to her knees and confessing undying love or something? She flushed. She must have given away something of her tumultuous feelings the night before, when she'd laid her head so trustingly against his chest at the hospital. How could she have been so weak? He attracted her, made her aware of longings she'd never experienced. She wanted him. But there was more to it than even that. She . . . cared for him.

She stared at her white face in the mirror. This wouldn't do. She had to get a grip on herself. She must fix breakfast and go to work and not let this upset her. She had Tad to think of, and no hope of a normal life as long as he was comatose. She had to think about Tad, not herself.

With that firmly in mind, she pinched some color into her cheeks and went back down the hall again. Ahmed was sitting on the sofa.

"I'll fix something for you to eat before I leave," she began.

"That is not necessary. I am not hungry."

She picked up her coat and purse. "Suit yourself. Goodbye."

"Are you not going to have your toast and coffee?" he asked suddenly.

"I'm not hungry, either," she said without looking at him.

She opened the door and went out. She felt sick all over. It had been bad enough before, when they argued. Now it was worse. He couldn't bear even to be in the apartment with her.

She'd only just made it to the steps when he opened the apartment door and called to her.

"What?" she asked stiffly.

"It is not healthy to go without breakfast when you are accustomed to it," he replied formally.

She looked back at him with glaring blue eyes. "I can take care of myself, thank you."

His face closed up. "Eat something at work, then," he said shortly. "Presumably you have a coffee shop nearby."

"I'll eat when I feel like it!"

His dark eyes slid over her like seeking hands. She flushed and he made an annoyed sound. He went back into the apartment and closed the door with an audible snap.

Lang came by her office at lunchtime. He perched himself on the desk and studied her with too much interest for a casual observer.

"You've been crying," he remarked. "And I don't need three guesses."

"He wants to get rid of me," she said furiously. "And I want to get rid of him, too! I hate having my cooking insulted!"

He smiled wistfully. "He's protecting you," he said.

She scowled. "What?"

"He's protecting you," he repeated. "I don't think he realizes it, but he's trying to get you out of the line of fire. He thinks you're in danger as long as he's around. You are, but we're Johnny-on-the-spot. You're both as safe as you can get. And moving him out of the apartment won't solve any problems, it will only create more. I told him that."

"What did he say?" she asked, trying to sound disinterested.

"That you mustn't be hurt, whatever the cost," he said, smiling.

She flushed. "How very nice of him. That wasn't how he sounded on the phone this morning."

"He's got a lot on his mind."

"I suppose he does," she agreed reluctantly, "with spies and assassins following him around everywhere."

"And his own bodyguard," he reminded her.

"That, too."

"You don't believe me, do you?" he mused. "You think I'm making up excuses for Ahmed, to keep you in our good graces."

"You spies are all alike," she said. "You do the job, whatever it takes."

"Well, I might have exaggerated a little," he confessed, "but not much. I still think Ahmed's main concern is that you might get hurt."

"That's not what he said."

He studied the fabric of his slacks. "Not exactly."

"What did he say, exactly?"

"That he'd be climbing the walls in another two days if I didn't get him out of there," he confessed.

"He won't be the only one," she shot back, infuriated. "He's driving me batty!"

He studied her flushed face, seeing far more than she wanted him to. He pursed his lips and smiled a little and she went scarlet.

"I'll see what I can do," he promised, rising from the desk.

"Thanks, Lang."

"Meanwhile, wear pajamas at night, will you?"

She gasped, horrified.

"He only said that you had a nightmare. And you were wearing a gown designed to undermine all a man's good resolutions and moral character."

"It was not!" she exclaimed. "It's just a common, ordinary, run-of-the-mill gown, and I never asked him to take it off me!"

Lang whistled and averted his eyes. She looked even more horrified. Her face went from scarlet to stark white and her hands covered her mouth.

"No wonder he's climbing walls," Lang said wickedly.

"You get him out of my apartment!" she snapped.

"With all haste, I promise," he said comfortingly. "Meanwhile—" he leaned closer "—wear pajamas!"

"I'll wear armor," she muttered.

He chuckled and left her sitting there, dreaming up ways and means of strangling her apartment dweller. How could he! How dared he!

She fumed all day long. When she got back to the apartment that night, she'd reached flash point.

"How dare you!" She exploded the minute she closed the door behind her.

Ahmed raised both eyebrows and pushed the Off button on the television remote control. "How dare I what?" he challenged.

"How dare you tell that Peeping Tom that I had on a gown!"

He looked stunned. "I said no such thing to him," he began slowly. "Nor would I have. The memory of it is a deeply personal thing, for the two of us alone to share. It would offend my sense of honor to divulge it to anyone else."

She stopped, touched by the way he expressed the memory. "But he said..."

"Yes?"

He looked dangerous. She hesitated. "Well, he said you wanted to leave here because I was driving you up the walls."

He smiled. "You are."

She was confused, and looked it.

He got up from the sofa and took away her purse and coat, depositing them on a chair. "Sit down and have some coffee. I made it. It is surprisingly good, for a first attempt."

She couldn't have imagined Ahmed making coffee. But he was right. It was good.

He sat near her and leaned forward, his dark eyes intent. "I told Lang nothing except that I dislike the risk of remaining here."

"Because of all that catered food?" she prompted.

"Because I find you much too desirable," he said solemnly. "You have no knowledge of men, or of the deceit even an honorable man can employ when desire rides him hard. It was dangerous, the way we were together last night at the hospital. You are vulnerable to me, and I to you. I have explained already how I feel about the situation."

"Yes, I know." She sipped her coffee. "Then if you didn't tell Lang, how did he know?" The coffee cup hung in midair. "Cameras...!"

"No," he assured her. "There are no cameras in the bedroom. I had my own men sweep it, to make certain. It disturbed me that you might be spied upon as you slept."

"Thank you."

"Where is the gown you wore?"

"I washed it and hung it in the window to dry." She caught her breath. "So that's how...!"

"A telescope, no doubt," he mused. "And there are microphones which can pick up a heartbeat from a great distance."

"Oh, dear," she groaned.

"Lang would not permit such a blatant violation of your privacy," he said, "and my men would not dare eavesdrop on me."

"I hope you're right. It nauseates me to think that someone might have watched, listened...."

His dark brows drew together slightly. "You know very little of the world," he said gently. "There are men who think nothing of..." He laughed. "Never mind. It is not fit talk for your ears. Drink your coffee.''

"I suppose you have your pick of women," she murmured without looking at him. "In your position, I mean. Diplomats travel in high social circles, and you're not bad looking."

"You flatter me."

Her eyes lifted, searching his impassive face. "I've never had much time for dating. I went out a time or two, but Mama was unwell a lot after Tad was born, and I had to help her look after the house, and after him. Most boys weren't interested in me anyway. I was always thin." She fingered the coffee cup. "After the wreck, I thought my hip looked horrible."

He laughed gently, without malice. "And now?" he teased. "What do you think of it now?"

She smiled back. "I think that you were very kind."

"I had a great deal more than 'kindness' in mind, Brianna," he said softly. "You are very desirable. I find myself lusting after you, and that is why I wish to leave here. An affair between us would be a tragic thing."

"There must be many women in your life who would gladly give you what you want," she said demurely.

He looked very introspective. "Perhaps. But it will be best if Lang can find other accommodations for me. This enforced togetherness will lead to disaster eventually."

"I haven't any plans to drape myself nude across your bed," she remarked.

He looked at her with lazy appreciation. "Even the prospect makes my head swim," he murmured. "You realize that I would find it impossible to resist you?"

"I would find it impossible to behave in such a way," she confessed. "I want to explain . . ."

The ringing of the telephone, an unusual event, stopped her in midsentence. She dived for it, listened for a minute and went deathly pale. She hung up.

"Brianna, what is it?" he asked softly.

"It's Tad," she said numbly, her eyes tragic and shocked. "He's gotten worse. I have to go to him...."

"You are in no condition to drive. Get your coat."

He phoned for a cab, certain that the agency had bugged the telephone.

Sure enough, when they got to the curb, there was Lang with the limo. He packed them inside grimly and sped toward City General without a word.

Tad's frail body convulsed over and over again. Brianna watched until she began to cry. Ahmed drew her into his arms and comforted her all through it. He refused to leave her, even when the doctor came and gave her a sedative.

"How is she?" Lang asked when Ahmed reappeared from the room they'd given her.

"She is not well," he replied. "She has spirit, but even so much will eventually give way. The boy's condition is dangerous. He may very well die."

"And if he doesn't?" Lang asked.

Ahmed pursed his lips. "Then he may come out of it," he said with a smile. "This is what the doctor hopes. It is evidence of frenetic brain activity, which can go either way. For Brianna's sake, I hope the boy recovers.''

''When will they know?'' Lang asked.

''Soon, I hope.''

And it was. Minutes later, Ahmed was called in by Dr. Brown, who was laughing with tears running down his cheeks. ''Come and look,'' he said. ''Then I'll let you wake Brianna and tell her.''

He drew the tall Arab to the ICU, where a young boy's eyes were open and he was being examined by another doctor. He looked at Ahmed with fuzzy curiosity.

''He will recover?'' Ahmed asked.

''With treatment and time, of course!''

Ahmed paused long enough to tell Lang before he burst into the room where Brianna was sleeping restlessly.

''Wake up, darling,'' he whispered, unaware that he'd even used the word. ''Wake up, let me tell you.''

She opened her eyes heavily, peering at him through a fog of tranquilizers. ''What is it? He's gone?'' she asked suddenly, choking on the word.

''No! He's awake. He's come out of the coma, Brianna. He's going to be all right!''

She sat up, clinging to Ahmed's strength while she fought to be lucid. ''Tad's all right,'' she echoed. ''Oh, thank God!''

He held her while she cried, then helped her as she struggled to get to her feet.

NO COST! NO OBLIGATION TO BUY!
NO PURCHASE NECESSARY!

PLAY "LUCKY 7"
AND GET AS MANY AS FIVE FREE GIFTS . .

HOW TO PLAY:

1. With a coin, carefully scratch off the silver box at the right. This makes you eligible to receive two or more free books, and possibly another gift, depending on what is revealed beneath the scratch-off area.

2. Send back this card and you'll receive brand-new Silhouette Romance™ novels. These books have a cover price of $2.75 each, but they are yours to keep absolutely free.

3. There's no catch. You're under no obligation to buy anything. We charge nothing—ZERO—for your first shipment. And you don't have to make any minimum number of purchases—not even one!

4. The fact is thousands of readers enjoy receiving books by mail from the Silhouette Reader Service™ months before they're available in stores. They like the convenience of home delivery and they love our discount prices!

5. We hope that after receiving your free books you'll want to remain a subscriber. But the choice is yours—to continue or cancel, anytime at all! So why not take us up on our invitation, with no risk of any kind. You'll be glad you did!

This lovely Victorian pewter-finish miniature is perfect for displaying a treasured photograph. And it's yours FREE as added thanks for giving our Reader Service a try!

**Just scratch off the silver box with a coin.
Then check below to see which gifts you get.**

YES! I have scratched off the silver box. Please send me all the gifts for which I qualify. I understand I am under no obligation to purchase any books, as explained on the back and on the opposite page.

215 CIS AK9W
(U-SIL-R-11/93)

_____

NAME

_____

ADDRESS   APT.

_____

CITY   STATE   ZIP

7 7 7	**WORTH FOUR FREE BOOKS PLUS A FREE VICTORIAN PICTURE FRAME**
🍒 🍒 🍒	**WORTH THREE FREE BOOKS PLUS A FREE VICTORIAN PICTURE FRAME**
● ● ●	**WORTH THREE FREE BOOKS**
🔔 🔔 🍒	**WORTH TWO FREE BOOKS**

Offer limited to one per household and not valid to current Silhouette Romance™ subscribers. All orders subject to approval.
© 1990 HARLEQUIN ENTERPRISES LIMITED   **PRINTED IN U.S.A.**

THE SILHOUETTE READER SERVICE™: HERE'S HOW IT WORKS

Accepting free books places you under no obligation to buy anything. You may keep the books and gift and return the shipping statement marked "cancel." If you do not cancel, about a month later we will send you 6 additional novels, and bill you just $1.99 each plus 25¢ delivery and applicable sales tax, if any.* That's the complete price, and—compared to cover prices of $2.75 each—quite a bargain! You may cancel at any time, but if you choose to continue, every month we'll send you 6 more books, which you may either purchase at the discount price … or return at our expense and cancel your subscription.

*Terms and prices subject to change without notice. Sales tax applicable in N.Y.

If offer card is missing, write to: Silhouette Reader Service, 3010 Walden Ave., P.O. Box 1867, Buffalo, NY 14269-1867

BUSINESS REPLY MAIL
FIRST CLASS MAIL   PERMIT NO. 717   BUFFALO, NY

POSTAGE WILL BE PAID BY ADDRESSEE

SILHOUETTE READER SERVICE
3010 WALDEN AVE
PO BOX 1867
BUFFALO NY 14240-9952

NO POSTAGE
NECESSARY
IF MAILED
IN THE
UNITED STATES

"Steady, darling," he said gently. "You'll keel over." He helped her into her shoes, unaware of the endearments he was whispering to her.

She leaned on his arm and walked into the ICU, dazed and stunned and deliriously happy when she saw Tad's blue eyes sparkle with sudden recognition.

"Sis . . . ter?" he whispered.

His voice sounded strange. It was the long period of disuse, Dr. Brown assured her.

"Tad," Brianna whispered back, smoothing his dark hair. "I love you, Tad."

"Love you," he managed to say. "Mom? Dad?"

She looked, anguished, at the doctor. He nodded solemnly. She looked back at Tad, forming words she didn't want to speak. "We lost them both. I'm so sorry."

He began to cry. The sound was haunting. Brianna had had three years to cope with the loss, but to Tad, they were only minutes beyond the terrible wreck. He sobbed, shaking all over, and Brianna gathered him up as best she could with all the tubes and wires, and held him, murmuring comforting words.

When he was calm again, she laid him back down and dried his tears.

"We still have each other," she told him. "You can come home and live with me. We'll be fine, Tad. Really we will."

"Head hurts," he murmured.

"We can give you something for that," Dr. Brown said.

"No!" Tad grabbed the doctor's hand. "Mustn't!"

"Don't worry," Dr. Brown said gently. "You won't go under again. You have to trust me."

He looked at Brianna, terrified. She nodded. "It's all right. None of us wants to lose you now. It's been such a long time, Tad. I've come every other day to see you. I've hardly missed a day at all."

"I know." He frowned. "Remember...your voice."

She laughed, delighted. "I told you," she said to Dr. Brown.

"Who is he?" Tad asked, looking at Ahmed. "Saw him ... through the glass."

"This is, uh, Pedro," she stammered. "He's a cousin of ours. From Chihuahua," she added helpfully.

"No cousins...in Chihuahua," he murmured.

"Oh, now, Tad, you remember Uncle Gonzales, don't you, who married Aunt Margie?" She bit her lower lip.

"Don't remember...much," he confessed.

She relaxed. "You will," she promised. "For now, you need to get some rest. Tad, it's so good to have you back!"

"Good...to be back." He smiled and closed his eyes.

She looked quickly at Dr. Brown.

"He'll be all right," he assured her. "Don't look like that. He'll be fine!"

"You're sure?"

"I'm sure." He looked at Ahmed. "Take her home, young man, and give her two of these. She'll sleep. She needs to," He handed Ahmed the tablets.

"I shall see that she does," Ahmed assured him. He drew Brianna to his side and along the wall to the elevator.

She let him take her down to the car, where Lang was waiting, beaming. He'd already talked to the doctor. Brianna listened to the conversation, but she was too muzzy and exhausted to register much of it.

When they got to the apartment, Lang left them at the door. Ahmed herded her inside and gave her the tablets, making sure she swallowed them down with a glass of water.

"Thank you," she whispered.

He smiled at her. "For what?"

"For all you did."

"I did nothing."

"That's what you think." She knew the tablets would take several minutes to take effect, but she was already drowsy. "I'll see you tomorrow."

"Certainly. Sleep well."

She nodded, wandering down the hall to her room. She closed the door and walked to the bed, and passed out on it.

Ahmed found her sprawled there minutes later when he looked in on her.

He chuckled. It seemed to be his role in life to play valet to her. He removed her clothes and put her into her gown. He almost removed her briefs as well, but that would probably send her into hysterics, he decided, when she woke. He slid her under the covers and pulled them up over her.

Her sleeping face was very vulnerable. He studied her in silence, watching her lips part as she breathed. She looked so fragile like this, and he felt guilty for being a burden to her during his occupancy. He'd have to be more patient.

There was, of course, no hope of leaving the apartment now. She would need someone with her, and Tad would be coming home soon. He would be needed.

That was a new, and strange feeling. No one had ever really needed him before on a personal level. He found himself feeling protective of not only Brianna, but of her young brother, as well. Odd feelings for a man in his position.

Well, he could sort them out tomorrow. He started to rise, but Brianna caught his arm and pulled it to her breasts, murmuring something in her sleep.

"What is it?" he whispered.

"Don't . . . go," she said drowsily, her eyes closed. "Stay."

He chuckled softly. She was in for more than a few shocks when she woke, it seemed. He pulled loose long enough to divest himself of everything except his own briefs. Then he climbed in beside Brianna and curled her into his body. She flinched a little at first, at the unfamiliar contact with a man's nearly nude body. But after a minute, she relaxed and curled trustingly back against him.

It wasn't going to be the most comfortable night of his life, he mused dryly, but he couldn't remember a time when he'd felt more at peace. He closed his eyes. Tomorrow was soon enough to face the implications of what he'd just done.

Chapter Seven

Brianna felt a weight on her arm. She moved and fell even closer to a warm, muscular sort of pillow. She must be dreaming. Her hand moved over what felt like a furry animal. It paused and moved again.

"Careful, *chérie*," a voice whispered drowsily near her ear. "Such caresses are much too dangerous early in the morning."

She opened her eyes. A pair of liquid black ones smiled into them. She jerked up, shocked to find herself in bed with Ahmed. The sheet covered his waist, and his chest was bare.

So was hers, she discovered as the cover fell and she realized that she was nude.

She jerked the cover closer, flushing violently.

"It was your idea," he pointed out. "You felt that the gown was too hot, so you removed it. And, uh, apparently everything else. Then you curled into my body and went immediately back to sleep. I confess, I was unable to. I feel like a man who has been through the rigors of hell."

"The tranquilizers," she stammered apologetically. "I'm not used to drugs. They...sometimes make me behave...strangely."

"I did notice. You made a rather blatant request."

She groaned and pulled the cover over her head.

"There, there. I understand."

"I'm ruined!"

"Not yet," he mused. "However, if you are still of the same mind you were in last night, I find myself more than capable of accommodating you."

She groaned again. "Oh, don't!"

He chuckled, stretching. "It was a revelation, to feel you like that against all of me." He groaned softly. "I confess that I removed the rest of my own clothing, so that I could enjoy the silky warmth of you even more. It took all my willpower not to carry through. You were deliciously soft and sensuous."

She was staring at his face. "You mean...you have nothing on?" she gasped.

He rolled over onto his side and propped himself upon an elbow. "Not a stitch."

She chewed her lower lip almost through. "I have to get up."

He swept his arm toward the side of the bed invitingly.

"I can't . . . with you looking."

"How could I not look at something so captivatingly beautiful?" he asked simply. "You are a work of art."

She flushed. "Well . . . you mustn't look at me, all the same."

"Then you wish to have me get out of bed first, *n'est-ce pas?*"

"Please."

He searched her eyes with a deep laugh. "Delightful little wretch. Will you hide your eyes in your hands, I wonder, and then peek through them to see what a man looks like when he is aroused and needful of a woman?"

She flushed. "You stop that! I won't look!"

"As you wish." He threw back the covers and got up, stretching so that his body was taut and the muscles rippled all the way up and down. And Brianna, with her hands over her eyes, parted her fingers just enough to get a shocking, blatant view of him. Surprisingly, she couldn't manage to cover her face back up. She took her hands away, her heart pounding, her throat dry, and he turned completely toward her, letting her look.

"It is not something of which you need be ashamed," he said softly.

"Oh, my," she said on a shaky breath.

He smiled. "You flatter me with those big eyes, *chérie,* but they make it all the more difficult for me to practice restraint." He turned away from her and found his silk briefs and pajama bottoms. He slid them up over his slim hips and snapped them in place before he turned to look at her. The cover had dipped, so that only the tips of her breasts remained covered.

"Still so shy," he accused. "You slept with me."

She flushed. "Not . . . like that."

"We slept nude, in each other's arms," he said. "Like lovers."

"But we aren't!"

He smiled gently. "We will be," he said softly. "The prospect of it makes me dizzy with pleasure. You're silk and satin. Innocent and sweet and brave. What more could a man ask of life than such a woman?"

"I won't be your mistress," she managed.

"Oh, Brianna," he said tenderly, "never could I ask you to be so small a part of my life as that."

She was puzzled. Her eyes sought his and found only dancing mischief in them. "Well, then, what do you want?"

"What you whispered in my ear last night as you slept," he said.

"But I don't remember."

"You will, at the appropriate time. Get dressed while I make coffee. Tad will be awake and impatient to see you!"

"Tad!" She laughed. "It wasn't a dream, then!"

"No. Not at all. Get up."

He went out, closing the door behind him. She jumped out of bed and rushed toward the bathroom just as the door suddenly opened again and Ahmed stared at her with rapt delight.

"Stop that," she said.

He shook his head and smiled apologetically. "I couldn't resist. Hurry, now." He closed the door again.

She darted into the bathroom, embarrassed and excited. She had a new lease on life, it seemed, and Ahmed was part of it.

Tad's eyes lit up when Brianna walked into the new private room he'd been given. He looked much better, with some color in his cheeks, and his speech had improved, too.

"I feel like Rip Van Winkle." He chuckled, his voice a little rusty but much more animated than it had been the day before. "Hi, cousin!" he added, smiling at Ahmed.

"Good morning, young cousin," Ahmed said indulgently. "I trust you feel more yourself?"

"I feel much better. I was worried about Bri, though," he confessed, falling naturally back into his old familiar way of addressing her. "They told me she had to be sedated."

"I'm fine now," she assured him. "I had a good night's sleep and I'm all right."

"I'm sorry I gave you a fright," he said, wondering at her faint color.

"You can give me all the frights you want," she told him warmly. "It's so wonderful to have you awake and alert and talking to me. Tad, you're all I've got in the whole world," she added huskily.

"Not quite, *chérie*," Ahmed said from behind her, his hand gently smoothing her hair.

She flushed, looking up into dark, possessive eyes.

"When can I get out of here and come home?" Tad asked eagerly, changing the subject.

"I'll ask your doctor. I'll pester him five times a day until he's desperate to let you leave," she promised dryly.

"Thanks, sis!"

But it wasn't that easy to persuade Dr. Brown to dismiss the boy. He insisted that Tad stay long enough for more tests to be conducted, and until they were certain that his body could manage on its own. However, he added with a grin, if Tad's appetite was any indication, keeping him fed was going to be the biggest headache Brianna would have.

Since the night Brianna had spent in his arms, Ahmed was convinced that marriage to her would solve some of his most pressing problems. The major one would be his hunger for her, which grew by the day. He wanted not only her perfect body but her warm heart and brave spirit. The minor problem would be his country's relations with the United States. Surely it would pave the way for better ones in future if he had an American wife. The more he thought about it, the more convinced he became that it would be a wise move. The details could come later. Now it was enough that the decision had been made.

He drew Lang to one side while Brianna was with her brother.

"You must make haste to solve this thing," he told Lang. "I can waste no more time waiting for assassins to do their deadly business."

Lang's eyebrows rose. "Are you and Brianna at each other's throat again?"

"It is not that at all," he said. "I wish to go home and be married."

Lang was shocked and trying not to show it. "Isn't this a bit sudden?" he asked.

Ahmed waved his hand expressively. "I have waited most of my life. Now this assassination plot has made me aware of my own vulnerability, of the risk to my people if I die without issue. I tell you, I believe my brother-in-law is mixed up in this," he added solemnly, his dark eyes unblinking on the other man's face. "He is the only one who could move against me with such ease and with cooperation from bribed officials. No doubt he has made many promises."

"You mentioned that once before. We've acted on it. We have operatives making every effort to wrap it up quickly."

Ahmed nodded. "I hope that it will not take much longer. Now that I have made the decision, I wish to implement it as soon as possible."

"I suppose congratulations are in order, then," Lang said, thinking how hard this was going to hit poor Brianna, who was so obviously infatuated with Ahmed. The man didn't even seem to notice that!

"Yes. Another thing, we must have a larger apartment for the duration of this charade," he said. "If Tad comes home with us, and I assume that he will, the apartment she now occupies will not be large enough for the three of us."

"We have a safe house nearby...."

"Unwise," Ahmed said at once. "Even if Brianna did not find it suspicious, the boy might."

"You're right. An apartment, then, in a building where we have a floor under surveillance. Will that do?"

Ahmed smiled. "Yes. Thank you."

"Where do you plan to be married, in Saudi Mahara?" Lang asked.

"It must be there, obviously," the other replied impatiently. "The duties of state," he added sadly. "I myself would prefer something quiet and simple, but it would be unthinkable not to have all the trappings."

"I understand. Well, I'll get the ball rolling," Lang replied.

Ahmed's dark eyes twinkled. "You look sad. You are a bachelor, too. One day, perhaps you will find a woman who can make you happy."

"I already did," Lang said ruefully. "But being the brilliant fellow I am, I kicked her out of my life and sent her running." He laughed curtly at the joke he made and went in search of a telephone.

Brianna was so excited about Tad that she hardly noticed the passing of time. But Ahmed's curiously tense attitude disturbed her and when she could manage it, she maneuvered Lang into an alcove to question him.

"Ahmed is very quiet," she told him. "Has something happened that I should know about?"

He ground his teeth together. "Sure you want to hear it?" he asked.

"I've got Tad back," she replied simply. "I think I can take anything now."

"I hope so. He—" he nodded toward Ahmed, who was reading a magazine in the waiting room beyond the hall "—is impatient to go home and get married."

Get married. *Get married.* Brianna heard the words with every heartbeat. She hadn't realized until that moment how much Ahmed meant to her. Now it dawned on her that he would certainly need to marry a woman from his own country. He was a high cabinet official. Of course! How would it look if he married a foreigner? How could she have been so stupidly blind!

"I see," she managed to say through a tight throat. She even smiled at a concerned Lang. "I've been living in dreams, haven't I, Lang?"

He grimaced. "Brianna, I wish..."

"It's all right," she assured him numbly. "I've been expecting it. Good heavens—" she laughed "—he couldn't very well get involved with an American woman, could he?"

Lang's eyes were sympathetic. "I didn't want to tell you."

She took another steadying breath. *Fate has given me a trade,* she thought. *It's traded me Tad for what I might have had with Ahmed.* She wanted to laugh hysterically, but it would not change the situation. She'd been a minor amusement for Ahmed. She'd been falling in love, but he'd been teasing, playing, while he planned all along to marry some woman back home. She felt like a fool.

"I need to go and see about Tad."

"Time does heal things, somewhat," he remarked, his hands deep in his pockets and a sudden, pained look in his eyes.

"I know." She touched his arm gently and then walked back toward the intensive care unit. She didn't look in Ahmed's direction at all.

She didn't change her attitude toward Ahmed noticeably. She was polite and courteous. But the distance between them grew, and he noticed her reticence without understanding what was wrong.

Lang hadn't told him that he'd mentioned Ahmed's upcoming marriage. But Lang had told him that they had an agent pretending to be Ahmed installed in a classy downtown hotel being very obviously guarded in his hotel suite. And there had just been an attempt on the man's life. Ahmed was concerned now for Brianna's safety, and Tad's. If he was discovered, all the red herrings in the world weren't going to stop the terrorists from striking at him; nor would they care if they happened to kill some innocent person who simply got in the way.

Ahmed, and Lang, went with Brianna every time she went to the hospital now. But Ahmed, sensing her withdrawal, didn't come any closer. He was protective and tender, but not amorous. Not at all. She wasn't sure if she should be hurt or grateful. After all, he had somebody else, and he hadn't even been honest enough to tell her.

Tad's animated presence almost made up for Ahmed's reticence. She delighted in his company, spent every available minute with him. And when the doctor said she could, finally, take him back to the apartment, she all but danced around the room with joy.

"I have already told Lang that we must have a larger apartment so that we each have a bedroom."

That wasn't all he'd told Lang, but she didn't say any more. "It might be wise" was the only comment she made.

He scowled. "You are withdrawn," he said quietly. "Since the night I slept with you in my arms, you have hardly had three words to say to me."

"I've decided that it was a mistake," she said without looking at him. "I don't want to get involved in a relationship that has no future."

His brows jerked together. "What do you mean, no future?"

She turned her head. "I think you understand me. I'm not going to be your plaything. Not when you've got a woman back home already."

He averted his eyes. "I am a man, full grown. I feel the occasional need for a woman in my bed. I will not apologize for being human."

"I didn't ask you for an apology," she returned. "I simply said that I'm not standing in for another woman."

"There would be no question of that."

"Good. I'm glad we understand each other." She put the car into gear and drove home, with Ahmed quiet and contemplative beside her. He'd already started planning a state wedding, and here was Brianna all upset about his mistress and refusing him. He'd already telephoned to tell the woman back home that he was marrying. He'd given her a handsome compensation and provided for her old age, and they parted friends. But apparently Brianna couldn't accept that he had a past. It made him sad. He'd thought her more forgiving than that.

And she still didn't know it all. Inwardly he was remembering just how great a deception he and Lang had worked on Brianna. There was a truth she hadn't yet discovered, one that would certainly have changed their relationship or even killed it once she knew. He hadn't wanted to tell her. He'd planned to wait, to find the right words, the right time. But she seemed unwilling to even speak of a future with him now. He'd waited too long.

He looked at her sadly. She was very young, of course. Perhaps he expected too much, too soon. He would have to bide his time and hope that she wasn't as unaffected as she seemed.

By the next day, Lang had found them a new apartment. It took all of a day to have everything moved into it by Ahmed's friends. Brianna was shocked at the way he did things, literally snapping his fingers to get people to do what he wanted. She'd never been exposed to anyone with such a sense of power and confidence. She stood in awe of him, but she was determined not to let it show. The woman back home was welcome to him, she told herself. She didn't want him!

While she unpacked, Ahmed spoke privately with Lang. "The boy will be safe here with us?" he asked worriedly. "I would not have him hurt now for all the world."

"He won't be," Lang said. "You'll all be as safe here as you would be in a bomb shelter twenty stories down. You're completely surrounded. There are bugs and cameras everywhere," he added meaningfully. "For your own protection. Remember them."

"Do you think I might need to remember them?" Ahmed laughed heavily. "She has no interest in me now that her brother is conscious. I have become the forgotten man."

Lang couldn't help but feel that it was the best thing to happen, since Ahmed was making marriage plans.

"I'm sorry. I know how you feel," Lang replied, and his eyes were distant. "I've had years of being the forgotten man."

Ahmed scowled, curious. Lang looked very different when he spoke that way.

"There was a girl back home," he told the Arab wryly. "I made a mistake. I tried to apologize, but it was too late. Now I can't get near her. She hates me."

"I am truly sorry."

"Me, too," Lang replied. He got to his feet. "Life goes on. I'll leave you to it. We'll be somewhere close when you bring the boy here. No more catered meals," he added.

Ahmed raised both hands. "Very well. I suppose that in an emergency I can learn to eat cursed hot dogs." He glowered at Lang. "My counterpart enjoys filet mignon and cherry crepes jubilee nightly, I suppose?"

Lang chuckled. "One of the perks of his 'position.'"

"Yes. Well, tell him not to enjoy it too much," came the haughty reply. "His position is very temporary indeed."

"He certainly hopes so," Lang informed him. "We're very close to a solution. I can't tell you any more than that. And I'm sorry to add that you were right to suspect your brother-in-law."

"And what of my sister?" he asked solemnly.

"I don't know yet."

Ahmed was preoccupied as he rode with Brianna to the hospital to get an exhilarated Tad that very afternoon. Brianna was apparently in high spirits. Her boss had given her the day off, and the women in the office had gone in together to get a special present for Tad. They hadn't told her what it was. They'd wrapped it up, and it was very big. She was as curious as Tad about the contents.

"I would have brought it with me," she told Tad, "but the box wouldn't fit in here with the three of us."

"Unsurprising," Ahmed said with disgust, looking around him. "I do not fit in here."

"You'll have to ask your boss for a raise, Bri, so we can get a better car," Tad said.

"I like this one, thank you," she returned. "Once it's painted, it's going to be beautiful."

Tad made a sound in his throat and she smiled, but the smile never reached her eyes. Ahmed thought that he'd never seen her look so helpless. It infuriated him that she was willing to throw away what they felt for each other out of misplaced jealousy.

They unloaded Tad and his things and got him upstairs to the tenth-floor apartment. This one had three bedrooms and a living room, with a spacious kitchen. Brianna hummed as she worked, putting together a special meal.

Meanwhile, Tad had opened the suspicious box and let out a whoop.

Brianna stuck her head around the doorway to see what he had. She burst out laughing.

It was a collection of everything from a football helmet to a baseball and bat, all that a young man needed to join the human race again, including a Walkman tape player and several tapes to play in it.

"I've never heard of any of these people," he murmured as he looked at the tapes.

"You'll probably love them," Brianna said. "Marjorie bought the tapes, I'm sure. She has a son your age. She'll know what's popular." She frowned. "My goodness, Tad, we'll have to see about getting a tutor for you, so that you can catch up to your age level in school."

"That is easily arranged," Ahmed said gently. "Later, though. Not today."

She didn't look at him. "Of course not today," she replied. She went back into the kitchen and fixed a balanced meal worthy of Tad's first night home, with all his old favorites.

"This is great." He sighed when he'd cleaned up the very last of the chicken-and-rice casserole and the canned apricots and homemade rolls. "Bri, that was the best food I've ever had."

"You flatterer," she said, smiling at him warmly. "I'm glad you liked it. Your appetite is certainly going to please Dr. Brown."

He leaned back in his chair, studying Ahmed. "How did you wind up here, Cousin Pedro?" he asked curiously. "Did our aunt and uncle send you up here from Chihuahua?"

"Why, yes," Ahmed lied easily, and his eyes smiled. "To look for work. And I have," he continued. Lang had placed all sorts of applications from "Pedro" in strategic locations. But no one had called him about work.

"Sure." Tad smiled with some puzzlement. "But that Spanish accent of yours is the oddest I've ever heard."

"It's been years since you've heard one," Brianna reminded him.

"Well, yes, I guess so." He flexed his legs. "It's so good to be able to get up and walk. I don't guess any of my old friends are still around?" he added.

"Todd Brock is," she said, smiling at his surprise. "He calls every month or so to check on you. He has ever since the wreck."

"Wow! Do you have his telephone number? Can I call him?"

"Of course, I'll get it for you." She hesitated. This was going to present many complications. She couldn't let him tell Todd where he was, or who was living with them. She grimaced.

"You're worried," Tad said, suddenly curious. "You don't want me to call him. Why? What's going on?"

Chapter Eight

Brianna stood in the middle of the floor with a mind that refused to work. She couldn't think up a good reason to satisfy that suspicious look in her young brother's eyes.

"She has only just managed to reacquire you from the hospital after three long years," Ahmed said softly, smiling at the boy. "Is it not natural that she should jealously guard your company for at least the first few days you are back at her side?"

Tad colored and laughed roughly. "My gosh, yes. I'm sorry, sis. That was thoughtless of me, really!"

She walked over and hugged him warmly, her eyes mirroring her gratitude to Ahmed over Tad's shoulder. "I'm sorry," she said. "It's just that we've only just become reacquainted and I don't want to share you for a few days. So, do you mind?''

"I don't mind at all." His blue eyes twinkled. "Todd can wait."

"Thanks, Tad."

He shrugged. "What are brothers for?" he mused, and then laughed.

One disaster was averted. Brianna found it difficult to avoid the questions that kept coming, though. Inevitably Tad noticed how careful Brianna and Ahmed were about what they said, about going out, about letting anyone in. He was a sharp boy. He didn't voice any of his curiosity, but it was there in his eyes just the same. He had his own television in his room, and he was quickly and eagerly catching up on three years of news and new developments in his favorite subject, science. But he was giving his two companions looks that became more perceptive by the day.

"Tad is suspicious of us," Ahmed told Brianna one evening when they were alone in the kitchen after Tad had gone to bed.

"Yes, I know. It's a strain for all of us," she replied. "But it won't be for much longer, will it?"

"I hope not," he replied quietly. His dark eyes narrowed in impatience. "I long to be free of the necessity for this stealth and deception."

"So do I."

"You do not look at me anymore, Brianna," he said suddenly, lounging in the doorway with eyes she found difficult to meet. "You look beyond me or you talk to my chin. You avoid eye contact. Why?"

She deliberately dried a dish. There was a nice dish-washer in the apartment, but there were too few dishes for a load. She liked the feel of the warm soapy water on her hands.

"I hadn't noticed doing any such thing," she said defensively.

"Talk to me!" he said curtly. "Explain this violent change of attitude. Is it because you learned that I once had a mistress?"

She dropped the plate in the soapy water and fished it back out quickly, with trembling hands. "Your private life is no concern of mine," she said through numb lips. "You'll be going home soon, won't you?"

He shifted irritably. "Yes, I must, once this situation is resolved. I have responsibilities which I cannot shirk."

"We all have those, I guess," she said sadly. She washed the last of the dishes and let the water out of both sinks.

He jerked away from the door facing and came to stand directly behind her, so close that she could feel the heat and strength of his tall body.

"Have you traveled at all?" he asked. His warm breath stirred her hair.

She really should move away, she told herself. And she would, in just a minute. "Not really," she replied. "I've been to Mexico, but that was just a quick trip over the border from El Paso while on vacation with my parents and Tad, when I was in my early teens."

experience with kids from being the den leader. And

"Have you never longed to see other places, other countries?" he continued.

She could hear the soft whisper of his breath. Her body tingled at his nearness. She had to concentrate. What had he asked?

"Yes, I'd love to travel," she said huskily. "It's a big world, and I know very little about it. Tad would like it, too. But it will be a long time before that can happen. He isn't fit for long vacations just yet."

"He is young. He will recover swiftly now."

"He likes you," she remarked.

"And I like him, Brianna. He has character, that one. Like his sister."

His hands had gone to her waist, strong hands that tugged her back into the curve of his body. His cheek was against her hair, and he was breathing more heavily now. She couldn't move. She closed her eyes and savored the sweetness of the contact.

"What has gone wrong between us, *chérie?*" he asked quietly. "Why have you turned away from me?"

She bit through the skin on her lower lip and winced at the self-inflicted pain. "We're very different," she began.

"Different." His hands contracted roughly. "And yet, so alike in many ways. I am a Christian, did you know? I never accepted the Moslem faith."

"Yes, I remember." Her fingers rested lightly over his strong hands, feeling the roughness of skin and hair and the steely strength of them as they held her.

"I enjoy classical music, as you do," he continued quietly. "I would live a simple life if I could."

Odd phrasing, she thought curiously. "Why can't you?"

"Because of those duties and responsibilities I told you about," he replied. "Many people depend on me."

Her fingers had become involuntarily caressing over his. Her body throbbed with insistent pulses. She moved back toward him, a little stir of motion that aroused him viciously.

His lean fingers dug in at her waist and his mouth dropped to press hotly into the side of her neck. He nipped her with his teeth and, feeling her jump, slid his mouth to her ear.

"They have cameras and microphones in every room, even in this one," he said harshly. "Whether you realize it or not, that small movement which you have just made was a blatant invitation, one which I madly wish I could accept. But do you really fancy making love for the amusement of our hosts?"

She gasped and tore out of his grasp, facing him from several feet away with wide, shocked eyes. "You started it!" she accused.

He was rigid with desire and temper, his black eyes flashing, his fists clenched by his sides. "And you were an innocent bystander, led into sin?" he chided icily.

"You could lead a stone boulder into sin with a voice like that!" she snapped back. "I'll bet you didn't stop with one mistress, I'll bet you had twenty-five!"

His eyebrows arched. "Why should that matter to you? You have already stated, emphatically, that you have no interest whatsoever in my personal life."

"And I don't!" she assured him. Her blue eyes sparkled like sapphires in a face gone white with pain and hurt.

He said something she didn't understand. "What do you want of me?"

"I want you to go home," she said through her teeth, "and get out of my life!"

"Gladly," he agreed. "As soon as they catch the men who are trying to kill me!"

"Someone's trying to kill you, Cousin Pedro?" came a shocked voice from behind him.

He turned, and there was Tad, clad in pajamas and looking as if he'd been struck.

"Why are you awake?" he asked gently. "Could you not sleep?"

"Not with all the noise," he murmured dryly, glancing at his sister. "She never used to raise her voice at all, you know."

"Truly?" He looked at her, and there was something very speculative in his bold stare. "She raises it to me constantly."

"You should try to get along," Tad told him. "She's a nice girl, really."

"I know that, to my cost," Ahmed said with a speaking look in Brianna's direction that made her turn scarlet.

"Who's trying to kill you?" Tad persisted.

Ahmed grimaced. "It was a figure of speech," he began.

"No, it wasn't, really," Tad said, grinning. "We've got men watching the apartment from across the way with high-powered telescopes, and I've spotted two video camera fiber-optic connections. And the telephone's bugged, because I opened up the mouthpiece and looked."

The two adults wore equally shocked looks. "How do you know what a bug looks like?" Ahmed asked him.

"There's these old spy movies I've been watching on television," Tad explained. "And there's been an ongoing documentary on the CIA that showed about bugs and stuff. Gosh, it's so exciting! I hope you don't get shot, of course. But if you do, I know what to do for a gunshot wound," he continued, while Ahmed buried his face in his hand and chuckled helplessly. "I watched a show about the medical corps, and they showed real gory pictures of how they treat wounds. It was great!"

"Oh, Tad!" Brianna groaned. "You shouldn't be watching that sort of thing!"

"I'm not squeamish," he muttered. "I want to be in law enforcement when I grow up. Forensics, maybe. Did you know how much you can learn about a body from examining the skull?" he continued excitedly.

"I think you should go back to bed," Brianna said gently.

"I guess I should," he said with a sigh of resignation. He glanced from one of them to the other. "Are you going to start yelling at each other again the minute I leave the room?'' he asked politely.

"Not really," Brianna assured him. "I'm tired, too. I plan to go to bed very shortly."

"Okay." Tad stood in front of Ahmed, who towered over him again. "You don't have a Spanish accent," he said bluntly. "You speak English like Omar Sharif did in *Lawrence of Arabia.*"

Ahmed's chin rose proudly. "You are intelligent," he told the boy. "And not easily fooled."

Tad smiled. "Thanks. Does that mean I get to hear what's really going on here?"

Ahmed smiled back. "No."

Tad shrugged. "You win some, you lose some. Good night."

He went away without another argument. Ahmed watched his retreat thoughtfully.

"He would make a fine diplomat," he remarked. "He is both intuitive and observant."

"What a delightful occupation to wish on him," she said curtly. "Look at what it's done for you!"

He cocked an eyebrow, turning to stare at her. "You have a very sharp tongue," he remarked. "It has been many years since anyone, much less a woman, dared speak to me as you have."

"They were probably afraid you'd chop their heads off," she muttered.

"In the distant past, that might have been a possibility," he told her. His eyes grew intent on her flushed face. "You have no idea what my culture is like, even today, have you?"

"You've got lots of oil in your country and everybody wants it," she replied.

He smiled. "True."

"You have a king and a parliament, your country was created out of Arabia just after World War I, you import high-tech items from the United States and Western Germany, your universities are some of the oldest in the Middle East, and the majority of your people are Moslem."

He nodded. "Very good."

"We have a new set of encyclopedia that I'm still paying off. Why isn't there a photograph of your king in it?" she asked suddenly.

"Because of the increased risk such publicity would afford him," he said simply. "Our king has been the target of assassins before this."

The slip didn't get past her. "You mean they're after your king as well as you?"

He hesitated. "Well, yes."

"Oh, my. I hope he's well guarded."

"He is," Ahmed returned dryly. "*Too* well guarded," he added loudly.

In a nearby room, several dark-suited men with earphones almost rolled on the floor laughing.

"What do you mean?" Brianna asked with a frown.

"They have him in a hotel surrounded by bodyguards and security people, being fed very well. I expect when they let him out, he will be like your Old King Cole of fantasy."

She laughed. It was the first time she had, in several days. "Roly-poly? Is he short and stocky?"

"The man in the hotel is, yes," he returned truthfully.

"I don't suppose there are many handsome kings around." She nodded and turned away.

He quickly composed himself. "I have a chessboard, if you play."

"I'm sorry," she replied. "I never learned."

"I could teach you."

She shook her head. "I'm very tired. This has been a difficult week. For all of us," she added, lifting her eyes to his. "You look very tired."

"I am. Tired and a little disappointed."

"Why?"

He searched her face with eyes that adored it. "I had certain hopes, Brianna. They have come to nothing."

She stared back at him with curiosity. "This woman back home . . ."

"She is my *ex*-mistress," he said curtly. "There is nothing between us now."

"I didn't mean that one. The other one," she prompted.

He was very quiet. "Which . . . other one?"

"The one you're going to marry!" she said, exasperated.

His lips parted on a spent breath. He searched for words, but he couldn't find any appropriate ones. "Am I getting married, then?"

"You told Lang you were," she said quietly. She lowered her eyes. "He told me."

Ahmed's expression was briefly murderous. He looked around the room. "I hope he has no plans to visit the Middle East when this situation is over. I think he might look very interesting at the end of a scimitar!"

"Why are you angry with him? He only mentioned it."

"Only!" His eyes came back to her and calmed a little. She'd been jealous. Hurt, too, perhaps. Her recent behavior began to make sense. It would be all right. She wanted him. His heart felt suddenly light and carefree. He would have some very difficult arrangements to make. And then a quick trip to the altar was certainly in store, before anyone else could throw more spikes into his wheel.

He didn't stop to think if his plotting was fair to Brianna. He'd always done things to suit himself. He was doing it now. She would be well provided for, and so would her brother. She would adjust to life in another country if he could make her care for him enough. He was certain that he could.

"My marriage plans are hardly finalized yet," he said. "And the lady in question is unaware of my intentions."

"Does she love you?" she asked involuntarily, her sad eyes searching over his beloved dark face.

He saw for the first time what she couldn't hide, that she adored him. He smiled slowly. "Do you know, *petite*, I think she does."

She made a faint smile. "I wish you happiness, then."

He couldn't drag his eyes away from her. She was so pretty. He moved toward her, lifting her chin with his fingertips to study her sad blue eyes.

"Will you miss me when I go back to my own country?"

"Tad and I both will," she said hesitatingly.

"And I shall miss you." He searched her face with faint misgivings. She cared for him. But could she love him? He bent slowly toward her mouth. Incredibly, as intimate as they'd been together, he'd never kissed her. He wanted to.

But she pulled back. "The, uh, the cameras," she said discreetly.

He muttered something in Arabic and took her by the hand, pulling her with him down the hall.

"Where are we going...not in here!"

"It is the only place Lang is unlikely to put a camera," he returned, closing them up in the bathroom. He propped his hands on either side of her, where she stood with her back against the door, breathless and excited.

"I don't want this," she said unconvincingly.

"Yes, you do," he replied easily. "You think I am being unfaithful to the woman I intend to marry. It gives you a guilty conscience to consider allowing my embraces."

She didn't have to answer him. Her answer was plain on her face.

"As I thought," he said with a gentle smile. "You are so very young, *chérie,*" he added solemnly. He searched her eyes and then let his gaze drop to her parted mouth. "So young...so very, very young...."

The words went into her mouth as he brushed his lightly against it. She felt the warm hardness of his lips, the velvet tickle of the thick moustache. Then, slowly, his tongue probed her lips, parting them, darting past her teeth into the silky darkness of her mouth.

He felt her stiffen. He withdrew at once, and his mouth lightly brushed hers, teasing it back into submission. When she relaxed, he started again. She was totally innocent of such loveplay. He had to remember that, and be patient with her.

It was exciting to make love to such an obvious virgin. He smiled as he made her mouth lift to seek the deepening pressure of his. He felt her shy movements, the hesitant reach of her hands around him, against his silk shirt, warm through it as they sought contact with his shoulders. She came closer and he levered his body down into hers, using the door to hold her there while he maneuvered them into greater intimacy.

She wasn't protesting anymore. Her mouth opened to the darting sensual movements of his tongue. Her body submitted to the slow, blatant drag of his hips that let her feel the strength and power of his arousal. She tasted him, experienced him, as she'd never known another man. She gave him everything he asked for.

Even when she felt his long leg push between hers, when she felt him lowering against her even more, so that his hips were squarely over hers and they were as intimate as lovers except for the layers of fabric that separated them.

She made a husky, passionate little sound in his mouth, and shifted quickly to accommodate him. He pushed against her rhythmically, letting her feel how it would be.

It was almost too late to stop. He shuddered and she clung when he tried to draw away.

His lips moved against hers when he spoke. "For a thousand reasons, this cannot continue," he whispered unsteadily. "The pleasure is becoming too urgent, too sweet to deny. All I must do is loosen two fastenings, and you will know me completely, standing here against the door. Let me stop while I can. I am too aroused to give you tenderness. It will hurt."

She felt his mouth touching her face, gentling her, as he forcibly withdrew from temptation. He held her while he covered her eyelids with kisses to calm her.

She was shivering with reaction. But there was no shame in what she felt. Finally her eyes slid open and looked up into his, curious and shy and uncertain.

"You know very little of men, *n'est-ce pas?*" he asked huskily, searching her face with quick, sharp eyes. "Do you really think that I have experienced such violent, sweet desire with a host of other women? Do you think this is such a routine experience for me that I am completely unmoved by it when I release you?"

"I don't know," she said shakily.

"Brianna, once in a lifetime a man may experience something so earth-shattering and passionate, if he is fortunate," he explained slowly. "I have no wish whatsoever to turn our magic into a sordid tangle of arms and legs in a bed."

She flushed. "Oh."

"It is not sex. That is what you thought?"

"You seemed not to want to be close to me, after the night we spent together," she said demurely. "I thought you'd decided it was all a mistake and you only wanted to forget it."

"I went up in flames and all I thought about afterward was how quickly I could strip you and relieve the ache you leave me with," he whispered wickedly. "But afterward, it made me ashamed to want something so physical, when I knew how fragile and vulnerable you were in other ways."

"So you ignored me completely," she agreed.

"It was the only protection I could manage," he told her with a long-suffering look. "Now that Tad is here with us at night, and Lang has cameras in most of the rooms, it would be quite difficult to find enough privacy to satisfy ourselves."

"You did maneuver us into a bathroom," she stated.

"Where I came to my senses in time," he reminded her. "I care too much for you to use you, no matter how much you inflame me," he added. "I meant what I told you. A man must not allow himself to reach such a frenzy of desire when he pleasures a virgin." He traced her flaming cheeks. "He must become as the wind across the desert, slow and tender and caressing until she is prepared to receive him."

She felt hot all over as he spoke. Her eyes fell to his throat, where a pulse throbbed visibly.

"You still avoid my eyes. Why?"

"It embarrasses me, a little."

"When we have been naked together in bed?" he teased softly.

"We weren't lovers."

He drew her head to his chest and caressed her hair. "Oh, we will love," he whispered. "But not as conspirators hiding in corners."

"I don't understand."

"Did you think me such a rake, Brianna, that I could make love to you while I had a woman waiting at home, expecting to become my bride?"

She hadn't thought about that aspect of his behavior. She lifted her head and looked up into his eyes with quiet curiosity.

"Well, no," she confessed. "It did seem rather out of character. But Lang said—"

He put his lean forefinger over her mouth. "Yes. Lang said that I was impatient for this charade to be over because I wanted to marry. Indeed I do, with all possible haste, and there are more obstacles and difficulties than you can possibly imagine because of my choice of brides."

She scowled. Her finger idly traced a button on his white shirt. Under it, his heartbeat was quick and hard. He caught her hand and she held his eyes while she worked underneath it to unfasten two buttons, then three, then four. His lips parted as she reached inside the shirt and began to slowly caress the hair-roughened muscles of his chest.

"I love to touch you," she said unsteadily.

"Wait."

She lifted her eyes again. "Is it so uncomfortable for you?"

"Yes." He put her hand to one side, smiling ruefully. "I have no plans to marry a woman from my own country. Although it is of a certainty that the woman I marry must agree that the ceremony be performed there. I am a high public official. I cannot marry in this country in secret. Do you understand?"

"Yes. No. You said you were going to get married," she began.

"And I am. Oh, yes, I am," he whispered fervently and bent to kiss her hungrily.

"Then who...?"

"You, of course. Who else occupies my mind waking and sleeping...? Brianna, marry me!" he breathed into her mouth.

Chapter Nine

While Brianna tried to cope with what she thought she'd just heard, Ahmed made a much more thorough frontal assault on her soft mouth. She couldn't think at all. She answered his lips and her hands slid with waves of pleasure over his broad, hair-roughened chest, savoring the feel of his body under her sensitive fingers.

He groaned and lifted his head, stilling her exploring fingers. "You are killing me," he whispered.

"You asked me to marry you," she moaned, reaching up to try to capture his mouth again. "I'm saying yes...."

She kissed him. He half lifted her and deepened the kiss, making her knees go watery weak as the heat between them reached an explosive force.

"I feel I should tell you," a deep voice came from the wall beside them, "that we had to put microphones even in the rooms where we didn't put cameras."

Ahmed's head jerked up. His blazing eyes searched the walls while fierce and probably obscene words rattled off his tongue like nails out of an air gun.

"I won't have our translator work on that." Lang chuckled. "Congratulations on your engagement. Now would you mind getting out of the bathroom and breaking this up? Some of us are turning to strong drink...."

Ahmed caught Brianna's hand and pulled her out the door into the hall. He was raging mad, and she had to muffle laughter at the expression on his face. She was glad her name wasn't Lang.

"He did warn us before we embarrassed ourselves," she reminded him.

He was breathing roughly and his cheekbones were ruddy with bad temper. His narrow dark eyes looked down into hers. He said something terse.

"Will you teach me Arabic when we're married?" she asked with a loving smile.

"Only when Lang is in another country," he promised, glaring at the walls.

"I heard that" came plainly from another part of the wall.

"Go away, Lang," Brianna said. "I'm trying to accept a proposal of marriage in here."

"Yes, ma'am," Lang said, and there was a clicking sound.

She looked back at Ahmed. "Are you sure?" she asked. "There will be so many problems. Americans aren't well liked in your country, are they?"

"My people will like you," he said with certainty.

"What if your king refuses you permission to marry me?" she asked worriedly. "He could, couldn't he?"

"He could make it difficult, if he wished," he replied dryly. "But I can assure you that he will not. He will find you ravishing."

She knew he was exaggerating, but the flattery made her feel warm inside. "I hope so." She touched the loose buttons on his shirt. "We'll have to live in Saudi Mahara, won't we?"

He nodded.

"All the time?"

"Most of it," he said. "I travel in the performance of my duties, but our capital city of Mozambara is my home. I hope that you will learn to love it as I do."

"What about Tad?" she asked suddenly.

"He will come with us, of course," he said, as if he wondered why she should even have asked such a silly question.

"It will mean uprooting him. And myself. We'll have to learn other customs, another language...."

"You brood about things which will fall naturally into place, *chérie,*" he said, "if you love me enough."

She stared into his black eyes with building hunger. He seemed to be waiting for something. Perhaps he was as uncertain as she was about the future. "I love you enough," she said huskily. "I love you more than my own life."

He drew her close and bent his dark head over hers, his arms bruising for a moment as he realized how much she belonged to him, and he to her. There had never been a time when he had considered the need to have someone of his own permanently to cherish. But he was growing older, and Mahara would need an heir.

"Do you like children, Brianna?"

"Oh, yes," she murmured happily.

He drew in a long breath. "There must be heirs. It is my duty to provide them."

"It used to be kings who had to do that," she said drowsily. "Now it's cabinet ministers, too. I won't mind at all. I love little babies."

He winced over her head. She didn't know his identity. He was tempted to tell her, but she might panic. It would be better to wait until he could settle the resistance there would surely be among his high officials and even among some American officials to this match. She would only worry and perhaps try to back out.

He drew away and looked at her rapt face. He smiled. "We will overcome the obstacles, together," he told her, reassuring himself in the process.

She pressed close and inhaled the faintly foreign scent of his cologne, secure with the heavy beat of his heart under her ear. "I'm twenty-two," she said absently.

"Yes, I know."

She lifted her head, curiously.

"Never mind how I know." He bent, smiling, to touch her mouth softly with his. "Go to bed. It is late."

"I'm tired. But I don't think I can sleep," she said.

"Lie down, at least," he said.

"Okay. But I'm undressing in the closet!" she told the walls.

There were good-natured long sighs among the men in the room next door.

Lang was repentant when he came to the apartment the next morning. Brianna had a tight hold on Ahmed's hand so that he couldn't do to Lang what his eyes threatened.

"Sorry about last night," Lang said. "Really, I am, but we thought it would be wise to warn you while there was still time. We can't afford to leave even one room unprotected."

"The sooner this is over, the better!" Ahmed said harshly.

"All of us feel the same way, believe it or not," Lang said, and Brianna noticed then how tired and drawn he looked. "We haven't slept."

"Don't you take turns?" she asked.

He shrugged. "It's still twelve-hour shifts. Manpower is scarce for constant surveillance. We're a government agency, you know. We have to beg for funding just like everybody else, and sometimes the politicians get it in for us."

"Ah, democracy at work," Ahmed taunted.

Lang glowered at him. "Well, at least if we don't do a good job, nobody herds us into the marketplace to be decapitated."

Ahmed was affronted. "I have not decapitated anyone for a decade. We are a progressive nation. We even have protest rallies, just like the West."

"I remember your last protest rally," Lang commented.

Ahmed shifted. "It was unavoidable. They stormed the gates of the palace."

"What are you two talking about?" Brianna asked.

"Your new home," Lang replied. He fixed Ahmed with a steady look. "When are you going to tell her?"

"When I have overcome the diplomatic obstacles," Ahmed said quietly. "And ascertained that she will not be assassinated along with me on the way back to Saudi Mahara."

"Good point." Lang stretched, big muscles bulging in his arms. "Well, I'm going out for a cup of coffee and then a quick nap."

"Are there any new developments?" Ahmed asked.

"Several. You'll have company inside as well as outside tonight," he commented. He stared at Brianna, who was looking uncomfortable. "You and Tad are pretty nervy people. Think you can survive a stakeout?"

"Sure," she said. "As long as I don't have to shoot anybody."

He smiled. "We'll do the shooting. But it won't come to that. I won't put any of you in danger."

"How about yourself?" she replied.

Lang shrugged. "I'm used to it. It's what I get paid for."

"Despite your eavesdropping propensities, I should hate to see you hurt," Ahmed added.

Lang grinned at them. "None of us likes taking chances. We're pretty sure they're going to make an attempt on you tonight. We'll be ready. With any luck at all, this will wrap it all up. If we're successful," he told Ahmed, "you could be on your way home by the end of the week."

Ahmed glanced at Brianna. "Yes," he said slowly. "So I could."

She didn't understand that look. It contained worry and apprehension, and she didn't think it was just because some enemy agents might make a grab for them.

The day passed slowly. Ahmed and Tad sat together in the living room, going over some new science magazines that Lang had provided, while Brianna reluctantly went to work. Her mind wasn't on her duties, though. It was on the danger they were all in, and especially on Ahmed's proposal of marriage. She wanted to marry him. She loved him. But until now she hadn't had to deal with the complications of marriage to a foreign national.

On her lunch hour, she went to the local public library and checked out every book she could find that dealt with Saudi Mahara. It was such a small nation that she had to choose general subjects to find out anything. Then she got a book on Arab customs and copied a magazine article on women's roles in the

Middle East. This would give her some idea of the new life she was going to enjoy, she thought. It would be better for Ahmed if his new wife had foreknowledge of what would be expected of her. Not that she expected to wear a veil and walk three steps behind him, of course.

Ahmed and Tad were deep in a discussion of nuclear physics when she got home from work with her load of library books, and there were four government intelligence agents sticking out of her refrigerator.

She stopped dead at the sight of them.

Ahmed smiled complacently. "They have had nothing to eat since lunch yesterday," he explained.

"Oh, you poor guys!" Brianna exclaimed.

They turned and stared at her. One was holding a carton of yogurt. Another had a carton of milk. The other two were having a minor tug-of-war over a wrapped cheese slice. They all lifted their eyebrows hopefully.

"I'll cook you up a big pot of spaghetti and some garlic bread," she promised, dumping the books on the sofa and making a beeline into the kitchen.

"God bless you!" one of the bigger agents said fervently.

The others marched him out of the kitchen to let Brianna work. It was quick work, too. She had spaghetti down to a fine art. The sauce should have simmered for at least half an hour, she supposed, but those men would all pass out sooner than that. She handed them plates and forks and started dishing it up the minute she could combine the cooked pasta with the meat sauce. Ahmed and Tad managed to get a few bites, too, and while everyone was occupied, Brianna made a bread pudding for dessert. Even the crumbs were gone five minutes after it was taken out of the oven.

Lang arrived just in time for the dishwashing. He had a toothpick in his mouth, and the other agents all gave him accusing looks.

"What?" he challenged. "I had a fast-food hamburger. A little one, okay?"

They surrounded him. "We," the biggest one said, "had spaghetti and garlic bread, homemade and delicious," he added, addressing a beaming Brianna. "And for dessert she made us bread pudding."

"And you didn't save any for me?" Lang asked, horrified.

"You had a hamburger," the big agent reminded him with a grin.

"I'll never do it again," Lang promised. "Can't I have just a crumb of bread pudding? It's my favorite."

"Sorry. We ate it all," the big agent said. He didn't look sorry. He was smiling.

"Just wait until I have to write up this surveillance," Lang began.

"Oh, yeah?" one of the other agents said, with his hands in his pockets. "And what are you gonna say, huh?"

They all adopted the same pose. Lang sighed. "That you're a great bunch of guys to work with, and next time I'll bring four extra hamburgers back with me."

The big agent patted him on the back. "Good man," he said. "I'll recommend you for promotion when I get to be President."

"I wouldn't hold my breath if I were you," Lang advised. "You'd break the budget in a week, the way you eat."

"What did you find out?" another agent asked, and they were suddenly all government agents again, all business.

They went into a huddle. In a minute they began to disperse, setting up equipment and checking it.

Lang was very somber as he drew the three occupants of the apartment to one side. "We want you to act naturally. Do what you've been doing in the evenings since Tad came here. We've swept the place for bugs and cameras, and it's clean. Just try not to be surprised at anything that goes down, okay? One of us will be with you all the time."

It became real life then. Brianna had seen films of terrorists. They had automatic weapons and no compassion. They killed quickly, efficiently, and without mercy. She looked at Ahmed and Tad and realized that she could lose either or both of them in less than two seconds. Her face went white.

Ahmed pulled her close against his side. "This is no time to become fainthearted," he said quietly. "You must have the bearing and dignity of high office, even when under fire. It will be expected of you."

Because he was a high official of his country, she realized. She searched his dark eyes. "I'm not worried for myself, you know," she said gently.

"I realize that. Nor I, for myself."

She smiled at him. "I won't let you down."

He brought her palm to his mouth. "Cowardice is the last thing I would ever expect from you."

She beamed. "Same here."

"Could you stop exchanging praises and just go about your business?" Lang asked amusedly.

"Of course." Ahmed let go of her and went back to the science magazines he was looking over with Tad.

The boy was wearing a new pair of jeans and a white T-shirt. He looked healthier, but he was still pale and weak. Ahmed studied him, noticing that he was as game as Brianna.

"You make me proud that I shall become part of such a family as yours," he told Tad.

The boy smiled. "That goes double for me. Will we live in your country, then?" he asked, because he knew already that he wasn't going to be left behind when Bri married. They'd made a point of telling him so.

"Most certainly."

"I'd love to learn to ride a horse. They say there are no horses in the world like the Arabians."

"This is true," Ahmed agreed. "However, the horses I own are magnificent in their own right. They are bred in Austria, and I . . ."

The attack was so sudden that Brianna wondered for a space of seconds if she was asleep and having another nightmare. The front door burst in with explosive force and men in masks carrying automatic weapons were spraying everything in sight with bullets.

Ahmed pulled Tad to the floor in a spectacular tackle while Brianna dropped behind the counter as soon as she heard the explosion.

The exchange of weapon fire sounded more like firecrackers popping than like real guns. It was surreal. Brianna knew better than to dare lift her head. She curled up on the floor to make as small a target as possible and hoped that the government agents were accurate with those nasty-looking weapons she'd seen under their suit coats. She didn't dare think about Ahmed or Tad, or she'd go mad.

There was a cessation of noise. A clink of glass falling. There were quick, hard footsteps and then Ahmed and Tad were bending over her.

"Are you all right?" Ahmed asked quickly, rolling her over and gathering her up close. His eyes were wild, his face pale under its natural darkness.

"Yes. Are both of you?" she asked, her eyes going frantically from Tad to Ahmed.

"We're fine," Tad assured her, but he was pale and his voice was shaking. "Gosh, that was some . . . something, wasn't it?"

Brianna clung to Ahmed, shivering with aftershock. Those men had come to kill him. The bullets had been meant for him. She gasped.

"All clear," Lang said, repocketing his automatic under his jacket. He looked down at Brianna, his face still showing traces of ferocity from the ordeal. He glanced over his shoulder. "Don't let her get up yet," he told Ahmed.

"Haven't you caught them?" she asked fearfully.

"Oh, yes," Lang said, and there was something in his eyes that she didn't want to see. She looked quickly down again.

Ahmed cradled her in his arms and sat with his back against the cabinet. Tad started to peek around the corner but Ahmed jerked him back.

"No," he told the boy, and his face was unusually stern.

"Okay. I was just curious."

"Curiosity sometimes carries a high price," he was told. Ahmed looked down at Brianna's white face. "It is over," he told her softly. "All over. Lang told me earlier that he was in contact with my government. The perpetrators will be caught now. The coup attempt has failed."

"Your king will be relieved," Tad remarked. "Is he okay, do you think?"

"Oh, yes," Ahmed said absently, stroking Brianna's dark, damp hair back from her face. "The king has never been better, I am sure."

Later, when the devastation was cleared away and the enemy agents removed, Ahmed and Brianna and Tad were moved out of the wrecked apartment and into another.

Brianna had noticed stains on the carpet, but when she tried to ask about them, she was ignored.

"I'm not a baby, you know," she told Ahmed.

His smile was a little strained. "No. But I am older than you, and I have seen more. Believe me when I tell you that you need not know all of what has happened today. Trust me. Will you trust me, *chérie*?"

"Yes."

He brushed his mouth over her eyelids and left her with Tad while he moved out into the hall to talk to Lang.

"Well?" he asked the agent.

Lang was still high-strung from the experience. He leaned back against the wall, squeezing a hand exerciser to relax himself.

"I hate to be the one to tell you this," he told Ahmed. "But they've taken your sister into custody." He held up a hand when Ahmed tried to speak. "They haven't connected her to the takeover coup. They've only connected her husband. It was a preventive measure only. But you're going to have to go back with all haste and set things right. You knew that already."

"I knew. Brianna has not been told," he added. "She must not be. I need time to settle my affairs before I attempt to involve her in them. This, today, has been a salutary experience."

"It isn't the first time you've been shot at," Lang reminded him.

He nodded, looking darkly arrogant. "But it is the first time that she and Tad have," he replied. "For that alone, I have no regrets about the outcome."

Lang stared at the hand exerciser. "Assassination attempts are few and far between, you know. Your father had one. This is your second."

"This is connected to the same people, however," he said, "and they are now in custody. I must see what I can do for Yasmin. She would not try to kill me. I know this."

"Get a good lawyer," he was advised.

"I must," he said heavily. "Our court system is even harsher than yours, and we do not play dice with the death penalty. The ringleaders of this plot will be executed if they are convicted, and there will be no stays or appeals."

Lang whistled. "Harsh justice, indeed."

"The old ways are cruel," Ahmed agreed. "Brianna may not be able to accept marriage when she knows my true identity. It is regrettable that I could not tell her the truth from the beginning."

"That was our decision, not yours," Lang said.

He smiled ruefully. "Will it matter, in the end, who decided?" He moved away from the wall. "I will be ready to leave first thing in the morning." He paused, and turned back to face Lang. "Thank you for what you have done. And the others. Whatever they pay you, it is not enough for the risks you must take."

"We get paid enough," Lang mused. "The occasional pot of spaghetti and a bread pudding are icing on the cake."

"You are brave people," he said sincerely. "If your government ever fires you, you will always have a job in mine. I could use such a minister of justice."

"Ouch," Lang said, wincing. "A desk job, for a street man like me? Bite your tongue!"

"Commander-in-chief of the secret service, then." Ahmed chuckled.

"That's more like it, and thank you for the offer. One day I may need a job."

Ahmed leaned closer. "If you continue to put bugs in the bathrooms of unsuspecting people, I can almost guarantee it."

Lang chuckled. "I see your point."

Tad had trouble settling down for the night after all the excitement. He still didn't know what was going on, and he wouldn't rest until somebody gave him an explanation.

Ahmed took Brianna's hand in his while they sat on the sofa drinking coffee from the new pot Lang had scrounged for them. The apartment was furnished, but a coffeepot and coffee hadn't been part of the furnishings.

"Since you were forced to endure the unpleasantness with us," Ahmed told Tad, "it is proper that you know why. There was a coup attempt back home in my country."

"Not Mexico," Tad said with dry humor.

"Not Mexico," Ahmed agreed. "My home is in Saudi Mahara, a country in the Middle East. I have been in this country to represent my people in a contract for several jets from Ryker Air, the company for which your sister works."

"They needed a place to hide him until they could find the assassins who were trying to kill him," Brianna added, still a little shaky from the ordeal. "They thought that having him masquerade as a poor Mexican laborer, our cousin, was a good disguise, since everyone in the office knew that we hated each other. The last place any enemy agent would look for him would be in my apartment."

"You hated each other?" Tad asked, smiling. "Really?"

Ahmed looked at her with tenderness. "I was immediately attracted to her when she heaved a paperweight at my head. It was the first time in my life anyone had dared to attack my person."

"I find that hard to believe," Brianna murmured dryly. "You have a way of making people bristle, you know."

He smiled indulgently. "At times," he admitted. "But when I am at home, it is a crime to attack me."

"Your king must think very highly of you," Tad remarked.

Ahmed sighed. "At times he does. At others, he is rather disappointed in me, I fear." He looked at Brianna. "You have not changed your mind about marrying me?" he asked bluntly. "I saw the books that you brought home to study. There may be things in them that disturb you."

"They won't disturb me enough to take back my acceptance," she said firmly.

"You bet they won't," Tad affirmed, "because I want to learn to ride!"

She glanced at her brother, delighted to see the animation in his face. It made her feel wonderful to see him alert and alive and happy. It was like a miracle.

"Not just yet, however," Ahmed said somberly. "There is something I must tell both of you."

"Oh?" Brianna asked. "What?"

He studied their linked fingers. "I have to go home tomorrow. Alone."

Chapter Ten

There was a flattering look of misery from Brianna and Tad. It didn't really make Ahmed feel a lot better, however. He had no idea how Brianna would react when she knew what would really be expected of her. Marrying a foreign cabinet official might not be so difficult. But he was not that. His life was one of rigorous protocol and duty. Would she be content with such a rigid life? Would she be able to accept it for Tad?

He didn't want to think about it now. "It is only a temporary absence," he assured them. "There are some things I must deal with."

"They've caught the people involved in the assassination plot, haven't they?" Brianna asked perceptively.

He nodded. He stared at his hands. "One of them is my only sister."

She put her hand over his and moved closer to lean her head against his broad shoulder. "I'm sorry," she said sincerely.

"Me, too," Tad offered. "Gee, that would be tough. Why would she want to kill you?"

"I am not certain that she did," Ahmed confessed. "I think that it was her husband's idea and not her own. But I must find out."

"You didn't really answer me," Tad persisted, his blue eyes, so much like Brianna's, unblinking.

Ahmed's broad shoulders rose and fell. "The hunger for power creates madness at times."

"But you're a cabinet minister," Brianna began.

"I must make some telephone calls," he said abruptly, glancing at the clock on the wall. "You will excuse me?" he asked formally.

She let go of his hand reluctantly. He was keeping something from her. It disturbed her.

"Of course," she said automatically.

He smiled briefly and left them, going into the middle bedroom to make his calls. He closed the door firmly behind him.

"That isn't all," Tad said. "He's hiding something."

"Yes, I know." Brianna was worried. She didn't want it to show, but it did. "Oh, Tad, I hope this really is the end of the assassination attempts."

They had a quiet supper later that night, one that Lang and the guys provided—huge pizzas.

"This is our favorite food," Lang remarked, passing Brianna another slice. "We live on it when we're on stakeout. We know all the best places."

"You could have offered to bring us a pizza instead of a little hamburger yesterday," the big agent remarked to Lang.

Lang chuckled. "I fell asleep in the booth with half the hamburger in my hand," he confessed. "I guess I went without a nap too long."

"Poor guy," one of the other agents said. "You ought to get a decent job, you know."

"I tried, but only the CIA would hire me," Lang retorted.

Listening to their banter relaxed Brianna, but Ahmed was quiet and subdued. All of them, except Brianna, knew why he was upset. Even his standing would not save his sister's life if she was found guilty of treason. He hadn't told Brianna.

When the agents left, Tad went to bed, leaving Brianna and Ahmed discreetly alone.

But there was a new distance between them. He sat in the armchair across from her place on the sofa, looking terribly remote and sad. There was an aura about him that she remembered from their earliest acquaintance, when he and his entourage first arrived at Ryker Air. She'd thought then that he had a rather regal air, as if his position gave him great importance and he expected everyone to be aware of it.

"Are you sorry that you asked me to marry you?" she asked bluntly, her blue eyes worried.

His fingers idly caressed the soft fabric over the arms of the chair. "No. Of all my recent actions, that is the one which I regret the least. You delight me."

She smiled. "Will you have to be away long?"

He shrugged. "I do not know." He wouldn't meet her eyes. "The leaders of the coup have to be dealt with."

"Yes, of course, but why do you have to be there?" she asked, frowning. "Do the cabinet ministers act as judges in your country?"

He got up from the chair and paced restlessly. "You should study those books," he said, nodding toward them. "They will help you understand the way of my culture."

"I'll do that," she said. She smoothed her hands over her jeans-clad thighs. "It should be very exciting, living near the desert."

"It disturbs you, though," he said quietly, glancing at her. "It will mean many sacrifices. Perhaps you will not want to make them."

Her expression was unguarded, and looking at it made him feel wounded. He missed her already. He moved toward her and scooped her up against his chest, holding her cradled to him with his mouth hungry against her neck. "Do not look like that!" he whispered roughly. "I cannot bear to see you so! I am only thinking of your happiness!"

"Then stop trying to push me away," she whispered miserably. "You do it all the time lately."

"Not from choice," he said fervently. His mouth became sensuous as it moved up to her face. "I adore you. I desire you. You are my life...."

His mouth found hers and he kissed her very slowly, with a tenderness that was almost painfully sweet. Her hands traced his hard face, learning its lines, while she fed on the warm expertness of his mouth.

His hands went to her hips and lifted her gently into the changing contours of his body while he kissed her. She began to moan, moving closer of her own accord.

His fingers contracted, pulling, molding, and she shuddered.

He lifted his head. His eyes were glazed with desire, blackly glittering with longings that he could only just control.

"Would you, if I asked?" he whispered huskily.

"Yes," she said simply.

He stared at her swollen lips, her misty eyes. "I want nothing in the world more," he told her. "But I cannot risk the premature birth of our child. There must be no hint of scandal, no question of his legitimacy."

Her head was swimming, but the curious wording caught her attention. "You mean I mustn't get pregnant until we're married?"

He groaned. "That is exactly what I mean."

She cleared her throat. "Oh. I forgot. I mean, your country is much more rigid than ours about a woman's chastity, isn't it?"

"I fear so."

She moved away from him a little and managed a smile. "Okay."

He was trying to breathe normally, and failing miserably. He laughed despite his hunger for her. "Just like that? Okay?"

She colored. "I didn't mean it was easy."

"Nor is it for me," he confessed. "I want you very badly. But we will wait until the rings are in place and the vows spoken."

He bent and kissed her softly one last time. "Go to bed now. It has been a long and fraught day for all of us."

"Tomorrow will be worse," she said quietly. "You'll be gone."

"Not for long, I swear it!" he said huskily. "It will be the most terrible torment, to have to be parted from you even for a few days."

"How flattering," she said with a coy smile. "I'll plan a special evening for your return."

"Not too special, if you please," he returned. "We have our reputations to consider."

She reached up to his ear. "I'll have Lang come and bug the apartment." He made a threatening sound, and she burst out laughing, hugging him close. It was heaven, to be loved and in love. She hoped, she prayed, that it would last. If only there were not this feeling of foreboding.

Ahmed left the next morning, with his entourage surrounding him and Lang bringing up the rear. He and Brianna had said a quick and uncomplicated farewell before they left the apartment. He'd taken time to hug Tad, as well. But in his expensive suit, surrounded by his own people, he looked foreign and unfamiliar.

"He's elegant, isn't he?" Tad asked as they watched out the window. Ahmed climbed into a big white stretch limo with two of his henchmen, and Lang got into the front seat with the driver. They drew a lot of attention from people on the streets. It didn't matter now, the danger was over. Brianna hoped it was, at least. She was still worried about Ahmed going back to his own country safely.

"Yes, he's very elegant," she agreed.

"I think we're going to like living in Saudi Mahara," he said. "Is there anything in those books about it?"

She shook her head. "It's very small. They mention that it has a king, and they give some impossibly long Arabic name for the royal family, but little detailed information. It isn't what I expected," she added. "They're a pretty modern country, with industry and a structured society, and women are fairly liberated there. They're very European, in fact."

"All that oil money, I'll bet," Tad said. He sat down. He was weak, still, and tired easily. Brianna had telephoned his doctor the day before to make an appointment for today. The experience they'd been through had been upsetting, and Tad wasn't his old self yet.

"You have to see Dr. Brown at one," she reminded him.

"Do I have to?" he moaned.

"It's just a precaution. You aren't long out of the hospital. And yesterday was pretty shattering."

"Ahmed saved my life," Tad told her. "The bullets hit where I'd been sitting. Gosh, I hope nobody tries to do him in when we go to live with him."

"So do I, Tad," she said sincerely.

They kept his appointment with the doctor, who pronounced him well on the way to recovery.

Monday, Brianna went back to work, leaving Tad with an off-duty nurse—Ahmed's suggestion—and she spent her free time worrying about Ahmed. He'd telephoned twice over the weekend, but the conversation had been stilted and brief, and she felt inhibited trying to carry it on. He seemed to feel the same. His speech was more formal than she'd ever heard it.

The distance between them had grown so quickly, she thought. And Monday, he hadn't telephoned at all by the time Brianna had cooked supper and cleaned up the dishes.

Tad was skipping over channels looking for something to watch, while Brianna worked halfheartedly at crocheting a doily for the coffee table.

"Wow, look at this!" he exclaimed, pausing on one of the news channels.

Brianna looked up. There were uniformed men on horseback and some sort of procession in a Middle Eastern nation. At the center of the pomp and circumstance was a man in a military dress uniform with a blue sash of office across his chest, sitting on a throne while foreign dignitaries were presented to him.

"Why, that's Ahmed," Brianna exclaimed. "Turn it up!"

Tad did, very quickly.

"...looking very fit following an assassination attempt. His sister, the princess Yasmin, has been detained for questioning for some time. There is doubt that she was involved with the plot. Her husband's trial was brief and he was executed this morning. Questioned about the fate of the other conspirators, a spokesman for the royal house of Rashid said only that they were being dealt with."

The picture flashed off the screen. Royal house. Rashid. Ahmed, sitting on a throne.

Tad saw the expressions chase across Brianna's face. His own had gone pale.

"He's not a cabinet minister," Tad said slowly. "He's the king of Saudi Mahara."

Brianna's hands trembled and the crochet thread dropped in a tangle to the floor. *King.* He was the king. No wonder he'd been so well guarded. No wonder he expected people to jump when he asked for anything. *He was a king.*

"Do you think he really meant it, when he asked you to marry him?" Tad asked, putting her worst fear into words.

"How could he have?" she declared. "He's a king! He wouldn't ever be allowed to marry a woman from another country...!"

"The king of Jordan did."

"Many years ago—" she faltered "—and under much different circumstances. This...this changes everything!"

She got up and ran into her bedroom, closing the door. She collapsed onto the bed, tears running hot and copiously down her cheeks as she acknowledged the truth. Ahmed had been amusing himself. There was no other excuse for it. She had been a diversion while he was forced into hiding to escape being assassinated.

The telephone rang when she was a little more composed. She went into the living room, shaking her head when Tad answered it. He got the message at once, punctuated as it was by her red-rimmed, swollen eyes.

"Yes, she's...she's fine, thanks. Yes, so am I." Tad sounded nervous. It must be Ahmed. There was a long pause. "Of course. I'll tell her. Sure. You, too." He put down the telephone.

"He said to tell you hello. He wanted to know how we were. That's about it." He grimaced. "Oh, sis, I'm sorry!"

She bit her lower lip, hoping that the pain would help stem the tears. "Me, too." She got control of herself again. "Is that all he said?"

"Yes. I don't think he knew we'd seen the broadcast. He didn't mention it."

"That was a BBC feed," she said. "He probably thought it was being shown in England instead of here, if he saw the cameras." She went to pour herself a cup of coffee. It was cold. She grimaced and put it in the microwave to heat up.

"He didn't tell us," he said.

"I know." She glanced at him. "Maybe he didn't know how," she added. "It must have been very hard for him, trying to live like a normal person when he was used to servants and luxury."

"I've never seen a king before," Tad said, trying to lessen the sad atmosphere. "It will be something to tell my friends when I start back to school, won't it?"

"Yes."

"You didn't take it seriously, did you?" he asked worriedly.

"Me?" She forced a laugh. "Don't be silly. I liked him a lot, but then, I didn't really want to have to live in some foreign country and learn another whole way of life, did you?"

"No." He shrugged. "Well, I would have liked the horses," he had to admit. "And Ahmed was a neat guy to have around. He liked talking to me about science. He knows a lot."

"He has degrees in chemistry and physics."

"Well, that explains it. I'd like to go to college one day," he said wistfully.

She heard the microwave buzz and went to take out her heated coffee. "You will," she promised. Her eyes swept over his pale face. "You're a walking miracle, did you know? I'm so glad that I still have you."

He looked embarrassed. "Yeah. Me, too." He searched her face warily. "You feeling better?"

She nodded. She sipped the hot coffee. "If Ahmed calls tomorrow, I, uh, I'd rather not talk to him. Okay?"

"Okay."

But he didn't call the next day, or even the next. Affairs of state, Brianna decided, must have claimed his full attention since his return. She tried not to listen to the news channels, but the temptation was too great. She suffered through political news and medical news and disasters just for an occasional glimpse of the king of Saudi Mahara. Once they showed him in his robes of state with a falcon on his arm. There was a very pretty young Arab woman in a designer suit with him. Brianna saw her take his arm, and she felt sick all over when the newscaster added that the woman was the widow of Ahmed's eldest brother, who had died many years ago in a yachting accident. Her name was Lillah, not Yasmin, so Brianna knew that it wasn't his sister. He was smiling at the woman, and she seemed very possessive of him. That was the last newscast she watched. She knew then that she was being an idiot. Ahmed had made it quite clear that he wanted nothing else to do with her. She might as well start living her life again.

The first step in that direction was to get her old apartment back. Now, with just herself and Tad to share it, there was no need for elaborate living quarters. Fortunately it still hadn't been rerented, and she was able to obtain it at the old rent.

Tad liked it better, mainly because there was a young man who lived on the same floor who became his shadow and idolized him—Nick, the boy whom Ahmed had befriended.

Brianna was still sad, but as the days passed, she began to enjoy life again, although not in the same way as before. She couldn't complain, she told herself. She'd had an adventure with a king, and she had her beloved young brother back. She really couldn't ask much more of life.

At work, she was promoted to assistant status and given a job working for one of the vice presidents.

She'd hoped she might get to work with David Shannon, Meg Shannon Ryker's brother, who was a live wire and a delightful person. But instead, she was shifted to the office of the vice president of finance, Tarrant Blair, a rather crusty older man with a wife and four kids and a mind like a math calculator.

She didn't enjoy the job very much. Even less did she care for the way Mr. Blair treated her. He had no consideration for her time. He would think nothing of asking her to work overtime, despite the fact that he knew her young brother was home by himself, and when it wasn't really necessary. He had plenty of time to get his work done during the day, but he came in late quite frequently and spent an unbelievable amount of time on the telephone with his stockbroker.

"How are things going, Brianna?" Meg Ryker asked her one day when she'd stopped by the office to meet her husband Steve for lunch.

"Oh, fine, just fine," she lied. "I'm very happy about my raise in salary."

"How's Tad?"

"He's doing very well."

"I suppose the two of you are having a lot of fun catching up on the time you've missed together?"

Brianna grimaced. "We were. This new job requires so much overtime that I'm pretty well worn-out when I get home. It's challenging, though, and the extra money is wonderful." She smiled.

She didn't fool Meg, who continued to converse merrily until Steve showed up. Once she got her husband out of the building, she pulled him to one side.

"Why does Blair have to keep Brianna after work so much?" she asked bluntly. "Doesn't he understand that she's only just gotten her brother back from the dead, not to mention what she went through when Ahmed was being guarded so closely? And she still has not recovered from the aftermath of that situation," she added meaningfully.

He scowled. "Blair shouldn't require any overtime at all. He isn't the busiest man on staff."

"Couldn't you check?" Meg coaxed, tracing a button on his suit coat.

He smiled, bending to kiss her softly. "Yes," he said. "I can check."

She smiled back, her eyes adoring his face. "That's why I married you."

"Because I kiss so well," he agreed, bending again.

"Because you're so concerned for the welfare of your employees," she corrected, the words muffled against his mouth.

"Exactly." He forgot what they were talking about for the rest of the lunch hour.

But when he returned, he had a private conversation with Mr. Blair, one which he challenged the other man to repeat on pain of firing. After that, Mr. Blair no longer required Brianna to stay after work, and his telephone calls with his broker became a thing of the past.

Three weeks after Ahmed had left town, Brianna was almost her old self again. She'd put the whole situation behind her and was ready to face the future. There was a man in her department who seemed to like her. She wished that she could encourage him. But there was no sense of excitement in her chest when he looked at her. Wherever she looked, in fact, she seemed to see liquid black eyes looking back at her.

She felt particularly remorseful one Friday afternoon when she dragged herself into the apartment, looking as if she'd just lost her last friend.

"You're positively mournful," Tad muttered. "Honestly, sis, you just can't go on like this."

"I'm only tired, Tad," she said evasively. She smiled, moving into her bedroom to change into jeans and a loose, floppy, colored shirt. "How are the lessons going?" she asked when she rejoined her blue-jeaned brother in the living room.

"My tutor says I'm bright and eager to learn," he said mischievously. "And that if I work very hard through the rest of the school year, and probably the summer," he added ruefully, "I'll be able to rejoin my age grade next fall. They've done lots of tests. He'd like you to give him a ring and go by and see him one afternoon at the board of education office." He pursed his lips. "He's thirty-eight, single and pretty passable to look at. I told him you were a ravishing model-type girl with no bad habits at all."

"Tad!"

"I didn't," he confessed, grinning at her. "But you might like him."

"It's early days yet," she said, averting her eyes. "What would you like for supper?"

"Macaroni and cheese," he said immediately. He followed her into the kitchen. "I'm sorry about how it worked out," he told her. "I know you're having a hard time getting over Ahmed."

She stiffened at just the mention of his name. "No, I'm not," she assured him. "I'm doing very well indeed since Mr. Blair suddenly decided to do his work instead of talking on the telephone all day."

"I noticed. It's nice to have you home. But..."

She turned and ruffled his dark hair. "I like having you at home. I'm perfectly happy and well adjusted. Now get out of here and let me work, okay?"

"Okay."

He went reluctantly back into the living room and started to turn up the television. But the buzzer rang and he went to answer it. Brianna knew that it was probably Nick. She was banging pots and pans and didn't hear Tad's excited voice. She did hear the opening of the door a few minutes later.

"Is that Nick?" she called over her shoulder as she took a pan of rolls out of the oven and sat them on the stove, reaching to turn off the oven.

"No," a familiar deep voice replied quietly. "It is not."

Chapter Eleven

Brianna felt her heart race madly into her throat. She froze where she stood, afraid to believe what she heard. "Ahmed?" she whispered.

"Yes."

She turned, her big blue eyes wide and unbelieving. He looked drawn, as if the weeks had been a strain. There were three men with him, big, tough-looking Arabs who took up positions in the living room where Tad was staring at them in fascination. Ahmed was wearing an elegant three-piece navy pin-striped suit with a white silk shirt. He was impeccably groomed. But then, she remembered, he was a king.

"Hello," she said hesitantly, uncertain about how to address him. Did she call him "Your Majesty" or curtsy?

Her uncertainty showed plainly on her face, and he winced.

"I... would you like to sit down?" she asked. "In the living room...?"

"Brianna," he groaned.

She moved back a step, struggling for composure. She plastered a smile on her face. "Tad and I saw you on the news," she stammered. "I'm glad they caught everyone. And your sister, I... They said that she wasn't involved. You must be very glad."

"Yes." His voice was suddenly dull, lackluster. "Very glad."

She glanced toward the living room. Tad was talking animatedly to one of Ahmed's men, who was smiling and answering him very pleasantly.

"Tad's doing fine," she remarked. "He's catching up quickly with his schoolwork."

"And you, Brianna?"

"Oh, I'm fine, too, as you see," she said. The smile was beginning to hurt her face. "Would you like coffee?"

"That would be nice."

"Your men...?"

"They are content."

She fumbled down a cup with a crack in it and quickly replaced it, rummaging through the cabinet and her meager store of dishes to find something that would do for a king to drink out of.

He came up behind her, catching her cold hands in his. "Don't," he pleaded huskily. "For the love of God, don't treat me like some stranger!"

"But you are." Hot tears stung her eyes. She closed them, but it wouldn't stem the sudden flow. "You're a king . . . !"

He whirled her into his arms and bent, taking her mouth hungrily under his, oblivious to the shocked stares from the living room or Tad's voice intervening, diverting.

Tears drained down into her mouth and he tasted them. His lean hands came up to cup her face, to cherish it while he kissed away the tears and his tongue savored the sable softness of her thick eyelashes.

"So many tears," he whispered, his lips tender. "Salty and hot and sweet. They tell me, oh, so potently, that you love me, *chérie.*"

She felt his mouth covering hers, and for a few seconds, she gave in to the hunger for him, the long ache of waiting. But she couldn't forget who and what he was. She drew demurely away from him and lowered her face.

He claimed her hand, holding it to his chest, where his heartbeat was strong and quick.

"They showed her on the television," she said quietly.

"Yasmin?"

She shook her head.

"Ah. Lillah."

She nodded.

He tilted her eyes up to his indulgent ones. "And you thought . . . Yes, I see what you thought, this sudden color tells me."

"She's very lovely."

"She is not you," he said simply. He touched her face as if he'd forgotten what she looked like, as if he was hungry to look at her. "I did not telephone you because it is too difficult to make conversation over the coldness of an ocean. I had to have you close to me, like this, so that I could see your eyes, feel your breath as you spoke to me."

"I thought that once you were back home again, all this might seem like a bad memory to you," she said.

"I have not slept," he said quietly. "I have worked for the release of my sister. There have been charges and countercharges, and many members of the military had to be dealt with to prevent there ever being a recurrence of this coup attempt. I have been busy, Brianna. But not so busy that I could ever forget the taste and touch of you in my arms."

"That's nice."

He tilted her chin up, searching her sad eyes. "You said that you loved me enough to risk marrying me. Do you still?"

She hesitated. "Ahmed, you're a king," she said. "I could...I could be your mistress," she whispered, lowering her shamed eyes. "I could be a part of your life that way, and you wouldn't be risking anything. There are so many people in your country who don't like Americans."

"I do not have a mistress," he said gently. "I do not want one. I want you for my wife. I want you to bear the heirs to my name, my family, my kingdom."

"They would be half-American," she pointed out, worriedly.

He smiled. "So they would. How politically expedient. Not to mention the benefit of having an American wife in the complicated thread of international affairs." He traced a line down her cheek. "I have made the necessary announcements, calmed fears, outtalked adversaries and placated doomsayers. All that I have accomplished since I left here. And I have arranged our wedding." He kissed her shocked mouth. "Even the vice president of your own country has promised to attend. So has Lang," he added dryly.

"It won't be just a small church wedding," she murmured fearfully, gnawing on her lower lip.

"Stop doing that," he coaxed, his thumb freeing the soft flesh. "You will make it sore and I cannot kiss you. No, it cannot be a small wedding. It will be a wedding of state. Televised around the world." He kissed her horrified eyes closed. "You will have a gown from Paris. I will have them send a couturiere to the palace to fit you."

"A couturiere," she echoed. "To the palace. The palace?"

He brushed his mouth tenderly over hers. "I am a king," he reminded her. "Most kings live in palaces, unless they are very poor kings. I am not. My country is rich. My people are cosmopolitan and our economy is excellent. We have only the occasional student protest. Once we had to deport some foreign students, but we later learned that they were deliberate troublemakers."

"I'm just ordinary," she protested.

He smiled. "So am I. Just ordinary."

"I'd be a queen," she said, just realizing it. Her eyes were like saucers. "Oh, dear."

"And Tad a prince," he reminded her. He glanced toward the living room. "Can you really not picture him in a crown?" he teased. "He would have the finest tutors in the world, and the best education we can afford for him. Oxford, if he likes."

She wondered if she was dreaming. Her eyes slid over his beloved face. So much misery, so many tears, and now here he was and he wanted her.

"There's, uh, there's just one thing," she said jerkily.

"Yes?" His smile was tender, indulgent.

She looked up. "Do you...can you...love me?"

The backs of his fingers drew slowly down her cheek to her mouth, under her chin, her throat. "These words should be spoken only in the privacy of a bedroom," he said solemnly. His dark eyes held hers. "Be patient. I have never said them."

Her lips parted, because what was in his eyes made her feel humble.

"Say that you will marry me," he coaxed. "Say the words."

"I...will marry you," she answered.

He smiled. He kissed her forehead with exquisite tenderness. "Now," he whispered, "it begins."

She had no idea what it would involve to marry a head of state. She and Tad were whisked away to Mozambara, the capital city of Saudi Mahara, like birds on the wind, leaving everything behind and all the details of closing up the apartment and shipping furniture to Ahmed's men.

Tad was given his own suite of rooms and a personal servant to look after him. He was dressed in the finest clothing, had access to the court physician if he so much as sniffled, and a tutor was immediately engaged for him. His head spun at the sudden luxury that surrounded him. His every whim was immediately satisfied.

That worried Brianna, who managed an audience with the king to complain about it. They were never alone now. They were constantly chaperoned and protocol was strict and unrelenting.

"He's going to be spoiled," she moaned when Ahmed dismissed her fears.

"He should be spoiled," he informed her with a smile. "He has had a savage time for a boy his age. Let him enjoy it while he can. And please stop worrying."

She glanced around the throne room. It always seemed to be full of advisers and visiting potentates and politicians. "Can't we even have dinner alone together?"

He pursed his lips and his eyes were sensuous as they searched hers. "Another week," he promised, "and we can be alone together all we like." His gaze dropped to her mouth and lingered there. "I dream of it every night, Brianna," he added breathlessly. "I dream of you."

"And I of you," she said huskily.

He drew in a long breath. "Could you leave now?" he asked pleasantly. "You are quite soon going to have a visible reaction on my composure."

She cleared her throat. "Sorry."

She turned and left, nodding politely to several curious men near the door who smiled at her.

The days were long. She was fitted for the wedding gown, which was so expensive with its imported lace and specially made fabric from Paris that she thought privately she could probably buy a yacht for less. It was a marriage of state, though, and this was necessary. Everyone said so. The queen Brianna must be properly dressed. Queen Brianna. She shook her head. That was going to take some time to get used to.

She spent some of her time with Tad, and the rest daydreaming about her forthcoming marriage in the lush garden with its fish pond and flowers. Just looking at Ahmed from a distance made her heart race. Soon, there would be the two of them together, with no prying eyes. She grew breathless at just the thought.

The great day finally arrived. She was dressed and a bouquet of orchids placed in her cold, trembling hands. Tad smiled at her reassuringly, as richly dressed as the handsome bridegroom waiting at the huge altar in the church.

There were newsmen and cameras everywhere. And the crowds were huge. The people of Saudi Mahara seemed not at all unhappy to welcome their new American queen. She hoped that their welcome was sincere, and not forced by the many armed guards who surrounded the area.

She kept her eyes on Ahmed as she entered the church. It was the longest walk of her entire life, and she was terrified. The terror grew as she began to recognize some of the people in the front pews, people she'd only ever seen on television newscasts. But she made it, her nerves in disarray but her head held high and her carriage perfect.

Ahmed's pride shone out of his black eyes as she joined him at the altar. He took her hand in his and they knelt before the high clergyman who was to perform the ceremony.

Later, she remembered very little except that the beauty of it made her cry. When they exchanged rings, and then were pronounced man and wife, she began to cry. Ahmed cupped her face in his hands and looked at her with an expression she knew that she would carry to her grave, held in her heart forever. He bent and kissed away every single tear, while their audience watched in rapt approval.

It was a fairy-tale wedding. Brianna entertained congratulations from visiting dignitaries until her hand hurt and her voice began to give way.

Ahmed stood at her side, tall and proud. The festivities went on long into the night and Brianna thought that she'd never been so tired. It disappointed her to feel herself wilting, because she'd lived for this night, for her wedding night, for so long.

When he led her to the royal suite, which they would share, she was almost in tears when he closed the door behind them.

"Ah, what is this?" he whispered, brushing away the tears as he smiled gently down at her.

"I'm so tired," she wailed, her eyes seeking his. "It's been such a long day, and I want to feel excited and strong and . . ."

He stopped the words with his lips. "You are telling me that you are too tired to make love," he whispered, "and I know this already. *Pauvre petite*, the demands of state are sometimes a great nuisance to bear. But this is only the beginning of our time together."

"But I want you," she whispered shyly. "And I've waited so long!"

"As I have waited." He kissed her eyes closed. "I shall undress you, and myself, and we shall lie naked in each other's arms all night long. Then in the morning, when you are rested, I shall make love to you as long as your body is capable of receiving mine."

She blossomed under his warm, tender mouth, allowing him to remove the exquisite dress and the even more exquisite silk and lace things under it. He lifted her in his arms, his dark eyes adoring her silky skin, and carried her to bed.

"Oh, how magnificent!" she exclaimed as he put her down on the canopied bed. It was gold and silver, with geometrical motifs that added to the allure. The curtains were black with silver and gold threads.

"The colors of office," he informed her, moving to the dresser to empty his pockets and unfasten his cuff links and tie clasp. He glanced toward her, noticing her nervous fingers reaching for the cover.

"No, Brianna," he said softly. "Let me enjoy you."

She blushed, but she subsided back onto the bed. After a minute, the shyness began to drain away and she found pleasure in the slow boldness of his gaze.

He divested himself of everything except his briefs. Then he turned, facing her, and let her watch him remove them. He was aroused, and her body shivered as she stared at him.

"A nuisance only," he said amusedly. "I require nothing of you tonight except for your closeness."

She could never remember being less tired in her life as desire suddenly overwhelmed her. She couldn't drag her eyes away from him and as he saw her expression, his chin lifted and his eyes narrowed.

He moved to the bed and balanced beside her with one knee. Her hand went to it involuntarily and shyly, hesitantly, traced up it. She paused, her eyes seeking his.

He nodded. She continued, her breath catching when she touched him.

He moved down beside her and his mouth eased over hers while he taught her hands to explore him gently, sensuously. The lights were all blazing, and if she'd ever thought of making love like this, she would have been horrified. But the sensuality of his hands and mouth, the lazy movements of his body, made her uninhibited and wanton.

By the time he shifted her onto her back and his body moved over her, she was mindless and totally receptive to anything he asked.

He kissed her while he made himself master of her body, feeling her shocked gasp as he began to take her. Her hands gripped his upper arms fearfully, her nails biting into him as the stinging pain briefly overcame her desire.

He lifted his head and his body stilled. "In the old days," he whispered to her, his voice a little unsteady in the heat of passion, "the old women would hang the bridal sheet out of the window the next morning to show the traces of virgin blood that clung to it. I am not supposed to know, nor are you, but they will take this one away and hide it tomorrow, so that for all our lives together they can prove that you had no lover before me, and that our children are legitimate."

She swallowed. "It hurt a little," she whispered tightly.

He smiled gently. "That is natural. But what I can give you now will make up for it. Shall I show you?" he whispered, bending.

She felt him move, shift, and his eyes held hers while he did it, until the right movement made her body jerk and her breath catch.

He whispered something in French, and his mouth began to cherish hers. She had nothing to compare the experience with, nothing to prepare her for the sudden fierce bite of passion into her body. She fought him because it frightened her more than the brief pain had. He laughed and lifted his head to watch her as he forced her body into an explosive culmination that arched her back and tore from her open mouth in a husky little scream. Only when he felt her begin to shiver in the aftermath did he allow himself the exquisite pleasure of joining her in that hot delight of ecstasy. It was, he thought as it racked him, almost too sweet to bear.

He felt as if he lost consciousness for a second or two. He became slowly aware of Brianna's whispery movement under the weight of his body. He lifted his head and looked into her wide, curious eyes.

He didn't speak. Neither did she. Her eyes went down to where his chest lay on her breasts and back up to his mouth and then his eyes with something like wonder. She took a soft breath and then moved her hips deliberately, so that she could experience again the pressure that it exerted in the secret places of her body. She flushed.

He touched her face, raising himself slightly on his elbows, and he moved his own hips, his knee nudging her legs farther apart. She gasped.

His hand slid down her thigh and curved around it. Holding her eyes, he shifted onto his side and gently brought her into the cradle of his hips so that they lay still joined together in intimacy. He smiled and pulled at her thigh, easing her into the rhythm. In this position, she was open to his eyes and he to hers. They looked at each other in wonder, and then their eyes locked and he caught his breath at the pleasure he saw in her face.

"Here," he whispered huskily. "Like this, my love."

He pulled her hips into his and pushed slowly until she accepted him completely. She blushed at the incredible intimacy of hanging there, between heaven and earth, while she seemed to see into his soul.

"Ahmed," she whispered, drowning in him. "Ahmed, I love you . . . so much!"

"And I you," he said unsteadily. "With all my heart."

He shivered, rolling slowly onto his back with her body still joined to his. His hands smoothed down her back, gently pulling. His body tautened under hers with each slow, delicate motion.

"Sit up and take me," he whispered.

"I don't think I can...." she began nervously.

"You are my love. My life."

"And you are mine. But I...can't!" She hid her face against his chest, and he laughed with delight at her shyness. She was a rarity in his life. A woman with inhibitions.

"So shy," he whispered. "You delight me. Brianna, you...delight...me!"

As he spoke, his hands moved her hips, making her gasp, making her shiver with pleasure.

She felt his body pull and tauten. His jaw clenched and he arched in a sinuous movement that she found incredibly arousing. Her lips touched over his chest in shaky little kisses while his hands brought them both to the most incredibly tender climax of his life.

She bit him in her oblivious pleasure, and his short laugh was as much a groan of ecstasy as he gripped her bruisingly hard and held her to the rigid clench of his body.

She felt him relax suddenly with a rough shudder, and her cheek lay heavily against his damp chest. The hairs tickled her nose and she smiled wearily.

"Is it so good, always?" she whispered.

"I think, only when two people love," he whispered back. His hands made a warm, sensuous sweep of her back and he arched up to enjoy the silky feel of her against him. "*Dieu!* You exhaust me with exquisite pleasure and then, so suddenly, I want you all over again."

She smiled against his chest, lifting up so that she could look into his dark, possessive eyes. "We're married," she said with quiet wonder. "We can sleep together every night."

He smiled. "There will most likely be very little sleep obtained by either of us," he mused.

She traced the line of his jaw. "I like making love."

"I like it most of all with you," he said, sensing her quiet fears. "I never loved before. It is the most profound experience of my life to lie with you so intimately."

She relaxed. Her mouth brushed his and she lay against him, sated and weary. "Can we sleep like this?"

His arms enclosed her. "Just like this," he assured her. His own eyes closed in drowsy pleasure. And finally they slept.

Brianna found that there were difficulties despite her love for her husband, but none that she couldn't overcome with some patient tutoring and understanding. She got used to palace protocol and meeting visiting dignitaries' wives. She got used to the things that were expected of a queen, just as Tad rapidly adjusted to life at court. He grew and blossomed, and soon Brianna relaxed. He was going to be all right, just as Dr. Brown had predicted.

There was a grand ball a few months after their marriage. Brianna had a gown by Dior, reflecting the silver-and-gold-on-black motif of Ahmed's court. Her hair had grown long, and she had it pinned into an exquisite coiffure—one that, she knew from experience, would be quickly disposed with when she and Ahmed were alone. She wore diamonds and pearls, and the tiara of her rank, and she met with approving glances from even the most stern ministers of Ahmed's cabinet when she joined her guests.

She was dancing with her husband when she noticed an odd expression in his eyes. His hand on her waist was curiously exploring.

"What is it?" she asked softly.

He smiled quizzically. "Is there something which you wish to tell me?" he asked gently. "Something which you have perhaps thought to save until you visited our court physician?"

"Yasmin," she said, glowering toward a gleeful sister-in-law who was wearing a guilty but very happy expression.

"Do not blame her too much. She dreams of dynasties, even as I sometimes do." He pulled her closer, his eyes loving and warm. "Tell me."

"I'm not sure," she confessed. "I've been unwell at breakfast twice this week. And there were a few other things." She searched his eyes. "I didn't want to tell you just yet."

"Why?" he asked softly.

"I was afraid you might not want to make love to me anymore if we were sure," she said hesitantly, searching his dark eyes as her hand caressed his jacket. "I thought they might take me away from you...."

"Chérie!" He stopped dancing and bent to kiss her worried eyes shut. "They would have to kill me to separate us," he whispered fervently. "And as for the other... Brianna, I would want to make love to you if I were on my deathbed!"

Reassured, she smiled shyly. "Would you, really?"

"I find you a delightful pupil," he whispered. "Adventurous and mischievous and totally captivating."

"I love you!"

"I love you," he returned. His hand pressed slowly onto her flat belly and they stood staring at each other while around them, suddenly curious and then knowing eyes began to gleam with confirmed suspicions. Without saying a word, or making an announcement, everyone at court knew that Brianna carried the heir to the throne. And it was a credit to them, and protocol, that not one suspicion was voiced until the actual announcement was made some weeks later.

Brianna's little prince was born on a bright autumn day, and bells rang from the churches to signal the event. Ahmed stood beside her bed holding the crown prince Tarin in his arms, with a beaming Tad beside him. Brianna, tired but gloriously happy, looked up at the three most important people in her life with eyes that reflected her joy.

Sensing her appraisal, Ahmed turned his head and looked down at her. His eyes were full of wonder.

"He is perfect," he told her, while nurses fidgeted in the background and smiled at his expression.

"A king's ransom," she agreed, loving him with her whole heart.

"Ah, that is not quite so," he whispered, bending to lay the tiny child in her waiting arms. "For, while I love my son with a father's great pride, *you* are the real king's ransom, my darling," he whispered, and he smiled at her radiant expression as he bent to kiss her.

* * * * *

Be sure to look for Lang's story in SECRET AGENT MAN—coming to you from Silhouette Desire in January 1994. He's the MAN OF THE MONTH!

HE'S MORE THAN A MAN, HE'S ONE OF OUR

Fabulous Fathers

DADDY'S ANGEL
Annette Broadrick

With a ranch and a houseful of kids to care for, single father Bret Bishop had enough on his mind. He didn't have time to ponder the miracle that brought lovely Noelle St. Nichols into his family's life. And Noelle certainly didn't have time to fall in love with Brett. She'd been granted two weeks on earth to help Brett remember the magic of the season. It should have been easy for an angel like Noelle. But the handsome rancher made Noelle feel all too much like a woman....

Share the holidays with Bret and his family in Annette Broadrick's *Daddy's Angel*, available in December.

Fall in love with our **Fabulous Fathers!**

Silhouette
R O M A N C E™

Take 4 bestselling love stories FREE

Plus get a FREE surprise gift!

UNDER THE MISTLETOE

Where's the best place to find love this holiday season? UNDER THE MISTLETOE, *of course! In this special collection, some of your favorite authors celebrate the joy of the season and the thrill of romance.*

Available in December from

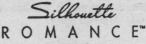

ROMANCE™

SRXMAS

SILHOUETTE® Desire™

It's the men you've come to know and love... with a bold, new look that's going to make you take notice!

MAN of the MAN Month

1994

January: *SECRET AGENT MAN* by Diana Palmer
February: *WILD INNOCENCE* by Ann Major
(second title in her SOMETHING WILD miniseries)
March: *WRANGLER'S LADY* by Jackie Merritt
April: *BEWITCHED* by Jennifer Greene
May: *LUCY and THE STONE* by Dixie Browning
June: *HAVEN'S CALL* by Robin Elliott

And that's just the first six months!
Later in the year, look for books by Barbara Boswell,
Cait London, Joan Hohl, Annette Broadrick and
LassSmall....

MAN OF THE MONTH
ONLY FROM
SIILHOUETTE DESIRE

Don't miss these additional titles by favorite author
DIANA PALMER!

Silhouette Desire®

#05715	THE CASE OF THE CONFIRMED BACHELOR +	$2.89	☐
#05733	THE CASE OF THE MISSING SECRETARY +	$2.89	☐
#05799	NIGHT OF LOVE	$2.99	☐
	+ Most Wanted Series		

Silhouette Romance™

#08819	EVAN*	$2.59	☐
#08843	DONAVAN*	$2.59	☐
#08910	EMMETT*	$2.69	☐
	*Long, Tall Texans		

Silhouette® Books

#48242	DIANA PALMER COLLECTION	$4.59	☐
	(2-in-1 collection)		
#48254	TO MOTHER WITH LOVE '93	$4.99	☐
	(short-story collection also featuring Debbie Macomber and Judith Duncan)		
#48267	HEATHER'S SONG	$4.50	☐
#48268	FIRE AND ICE	$4.50	☐
#48269	THE AUSTRALIAN	$4.50	☐

TOTAL AMOUNT	$	
POSTAGE & HANDLING	$	
($1.00 for one book, 50¢ for each additional)		
APPLICABLE TAXES**	$	_____
TOTAL PAYABLE	$	_____
(check or money order—please do not send cash)		

To order, complete this form and send it, along with a check or money order for the total above, payable to Silhouette Books, to: *In the U.S.:* 3010 Walden Avenue, P.O. Box 9077, Buffalo, NY 14269-9077; *In Canada:* P.O. Box 636, Fort Erie, Ontario, L2A 5X3.

Name: _____

Address: _____ City: _____

State/Prov.: _____ Zip/Postal Code: _____

**New York residents remit applicable sales taxes.
  Canadian residents remit applicable GST and provincial taxes.   DPBACK3

▼ *Silhouette*®